I0622048

# BANG

*Hard Hit #13*

## CHARITY PARKERSON

The scanning, uploading, and distributing of this book via the internet or via any other means without the permission of the copyright owner is illegal and punishable by law. Criminal copyright infringement, including infringement without monetary gain, is investigated by the FBI and is punishable by up to 5 years in federal prison and a fine of $250,000. Please purchase only authorized electronic editions, and do not participate in or encourage electronic piracy of copyrighted materials. Brief passages may be quoted for review purposes if credit is given to the copyright holder. Your support of the author's rights is appreciated. Any resemblances to person(s) living or dead, is completely coincidental. All items contained within this novel are products of the author's imagination.

--Warning: This book is intended for readers over the age of 18.

Copyright © 2017 Charity Parkerson
Editor: Hercules Editing and Consultants
All rights reserved.

**ISBN-13: 978-1-946099-27-3**

ISBN-10: 1-946099-27-9

❀ Created with Vellum

# INTRODUCTION

### Maksim doesn't do strings. Marshall doesn't date men. They're both about to be proven wrong.

Marshall is the golden child. He wins every game he plays—on and off the field. He's living the dream and knows it. That's why he refuses to let a thing like preferring men in his bed get in his way. Right now, he's all about his career. Everything else can wait, or so he thinks, until he meets Maksim.

Maksim has it all and basks in it. It's his job to check out sexy, talented men and offer them lots of money. Sometimes, they're extremely grateful for his services. What more could a man want? The last distraction Maksim needs is a relationship. Maksim never expects Marshall. Marshall teases, taunts, and tempts Maksim in ways he never dreamed. He also makes Maksim want a life he never has before.

Two men with no desire to change will have to find a way to bend or end up breaking each other.

# CHAPTER ONE

The night they met...

The club-level crowd was outrageous. When Marshall had agreed to show up at tonight's Blue Fires game, he'd only been thinking of his twin, Michael. Otherwise, he might not have agreed. Marshall was a few short minutes away from being highlighted on the Jumbotron in front of more than twenty thousand fans. He'd never been club level, but he played football in front of more than four times as many screaming fans, yet he was still nervous as hell. Maybe it was due to plotting against his twin, Michael.

Marshall followed on his brother's heels and prayed he wasn't making a mistake. A week ago, he'd unwittingly ruined Michael's relationship with the only man his brother ever loved. Tonight, he would stick his neck out and hope life didn't chop off his head while he tried fixing the damage he'd done. The love of Michael's life, Gavin, used to be Marshall's best friend. Now the man wanted to marry Marshall's baby brother. Yes, Marshall owned those two minutes he'd arrived into the world ahead of Michael. Marshall would smile and watch Gavin marry Michael—no matter his thoughts on the matter, because Michael was the only person—other than himself that Marshall loved.

"Hey," Michael called, snagging some dude's attention and dragging Marshall from the sickening sense of dread sitting in his gut.

The dark-haired man turned at Michael's greeting. His smile was luminous as he spotted Michael. "Hello again." Goddamn, the dude had a thick and sexy accent. "We're getting very good at meeting like this." His gaze slid over Michael's shoulder, landing on Marshall, before meeting Michael's stare again. Immediately, the man's almost violet eyes moved back to stare at Marshall "I don't wish to alarm you, but you have a man who looks exactly like you standing right behind you."

Michael snorted. A smile tugged at Marshall's lips. The man had a sense of humor. Sexy. Michael moved aside, making room for Marshall. He motioned

Marshall's way. "Maksim, this is my brother, Marshall. Marshall, Maksim Petrov. He's a talent scout."

Maksim held out his hand for Marshall to shake. "It is nice to meet you. Your face is familiar to me," Maksim said before laughing. "That wasn't meant to be the joke it turned out to be. I honestly believe I've seen you before. In fact, I'm already positive I'd like to see you again."

Goddamn. Marshall was certain he'd like to see Maksim again as well, and they'd just met.

Thankfully, Michael kept up their side of the conversation since Marshall couldn't get his tongue to work properly. He honestly believed he'd never met a sexier man. "Marshall is quarterback for the Land Sharks," Michael explained.

Maksim slid a heated gaze down Marshall's body, setting every inch of Marshall's skin ablaze. "Ah, that explains things. Would the two of you care to sit with me?"

Marshall's tongue magically came back to life. He couldn't let this man get away. "I'd like that," Marshall said, answering for them.

He could feel his brother's stare boring into the side of his head, but Marshall couldn't tear his gaze away from Maksim. The man wore an expensive-looking business suit. Despite his dark hair being slicked back, it kept falling forward, blocking the man's gorgeous eyes. Marshall had never been so instantly drawn to anyone before. Maksim led the way to a private table. Marshall watched his every move. He had the perfect ass. Marshall fought the urge to touch it. When they reached the table, Michael chose the opposite side from Maksim, leaving the chair beside the sexy talent scout empty. Marshall claimed it, incapable of putting any distance between them. In fact, he needed to know everything about the man.

"Where are you from, Mr. Petrov?"

Maksim winked. Marshall sucked in a breath to counteract the instant lust. "It is Maksim only. I am from Samara. It is the sixth largest city in Russia."

Marshall's smile was out of his control. He loved the man's accent. "I don't know much about Russia. Sorry."

Maksim's smile turned wicked. Marshall's gaze dropped to his lips. He craved every word. "If you'd like to learn, I'd be happy to give you a tour. It is a very beautiful place. Of course, it's cold, and you are probably used to the heat. I'm sure I could find ways to keep you warm."

Playing the fool was second nature to Marshall. He wasn't like Michael. Michael was the gay twin. Marshall was the athlete. They each had their part to play in life. "I've heard how y'all like to drink."

"Among other things," Maksim said, inching closer to Marshall. Despite all the warning bells clanging in Marshall's head, he didn't back away. The man's hair fell across his eyes once more. Without thought, Marshall's hand lifted. He itched to push the lock behind the man's ear. Thankfully, he caught himself before giving himself away. Marshall flattened his palm on the table, fighting his urges.

The man Gavin had told Marshall to meet to set their plan in motion, Shayne Something-or-another, appeared at the edge of the table, saving Marshall from himself. He handed Marshall an earpiece and another to Michael. "Put these in. They'll be announcing you soon."

Marshall shoved the tiny bud inside his ear. A voice chattered instructions in his ear and started counting down.

Michael held the earbud away from his body, looking scandalized. "Wait. Why do I need this?"

Shayne hesitated, making Marshall worry the man was about to ruin Gavin's plan. Instead, he rattled off something about them highlighting Michael too as Marshall's brother. Bitterness rose in Marshall's throat. Even though he knew Shayne had pulled out a bullshit excuse to get Michael to cooperate, he fucking hated when people made Michael feel like he was the other brother—the one who came in second.

So Marshall was the starting quarterback for the New Orleans Land Sharks. Who fucking cared? No one who mattered, that was who. Michael deserved equal amounts of respect.

Michael met Marshall's stare, looking desperate. "Why do I need this?"

Irritation with the unfairness of life had Marshall snapping. "Just put it in. We're almost out of time."

Always the loyal brother, Michael shoved the earpiece in just as the countdown in Marshall's ear came to an end, and his face appeared on the Jumbotron.

"Joining us tonight, cheering for his home team, is quarterback for the New Orleans Land Sharks, Marshall Frost."

Marshall smiled and waved to the sound of loud cheers. A sigh of relief rose in his throat when the camera moved Michael's way. "Also joining us this evening is Marshall's twin, Michael Frost, fiancé to Blue Fires Forward, Gavin Weeks."

There it was—the reason they were there. Gavin's evil plan to announce Michael as his fiancé in hopes of making it true. Michael waved before the news obviously sank in. Marshall watched his brother's expression shift. It was subtle. Most people wouldn't notice, but they were identical. Michael couldn't hide anything from Marshall.

Maksim shifted to his feet and grabbed Michael's hand to shake. "Congratulations."

Michael looked shell-shocked. "Thank you."

Marshall interceded before Michael made Gavin look like an idiot by admitting he hadn't known he was marrying Gavin before that moment. After tugging Michael into a bear hug, he pressed his lips to Michael's ear, ensuring no one else heard their conversation. "Stop looking so shocked. People might think you're unhappy. By the way, after what Gavin just did, I'm glad you didn't give up on him through all these years. He obviously loves you and that's all I've ever wanted—someone to deserve you."

"What just happened?" Michael's open confusion had Marshall praying he hadn't made a huge mistake. "Did you do this?"

Marshall slapped him across the back, managing to still play the part for anyone watching. "Nah. I just got you here. This was all Gavin. He loves you, Michael. You don't have to marry him. He'll be the only one embarrassed if you don't, but hear him out after the game. Dude loves you."

Before Marshall could say more, Maksim appeared at his side, holding a beer out for Marshall. "What are your plans later tonight?"

A jolt of panic ran through Marshall. He'd taken things too far. Given himself away. As sexy as he found Maksim, he needed to shut this down before he ruined his life and career. Even to his ears, Marshall's voice sounded tight when he answered. "How do you mean?"

Maksim nodded toward Michael. "Your brother will understandably wish to go home with his fiancé. Perhaps you'd like to go home with me?" The confidence in Maksim's tone had Marshall ready to do anything the man asked. His fear held him in check. Some things were ingrained too deeply.

He didn't reach for the beer. "I think you have the wrong idea about me."

Maksim's eyebrows rose. He did not have the wrong impression. Everyone standing there knew it. The gorgeous Russian transformed from smooth flirt to cold indifference so quickly the room chilled by ten degrees. "I see. You're a coward. How tiresome." Without another word, he walked away.

Rage had Marshall staring a hole in the man's back. "Oh, hell no," he said, going after the man who was quickly disappearing without a word to Michael. No one called him a fucking coward and then walked away.

Marshall handed off his earpiece to the first sound man he spotted before chasing Maksim down. "Hey, Maksim. Hold up."

At his shout, Maksim paused. His shoulders fell

before he spun, wearing a blatantly false smile. "Is there something I can do for you?"

Marshall felt his face harden. "You called me a coward, then ran for it."

"Have you decided you're not a craven after all?"

"I'm trying to decide how you getting the wrong impression reflects on me."

Maksim blew out a tired-sounding sigh. "Look, Marshall. It is Marshall, right?"

Marshall nodded.

The sexy Russian flashed him a bland smile. "Look, I don't care if you're hiding your sexuality. In fact, I don't give a damn if you're still lying to yourself. I have the best job in the world, checking out sexy men and offering them lots of money. You're not the first closeted gay I've met and you won't be the last. So don't lie to me, because I'll never lie to you. If you want to fuck, then say the word. No one ever has to know, and I'd show you the time of your life. Otherwise, I see a very sexy musician who I know for a fact loves rope play."

The knot in the pit of Marshall's stomach was a small thing when compared to his self-hatred. Maksim was offering Marshall a night he wouldn't forget, and Marshall wasn't brave enough to take it.

"Like I said, I think I've given you the wrong impression."

An ugly smirk touched Maksim's sexy lips. "That's too bad. I would've rocked your world. No strings attached, of course," Maksim snorted, "since I don't do strings. It's been nice meeting you, Marshall." Maksim said his name as if he still wasn't sure Marshall was the right name. Yet Maksim obviously had no problem remembering Michael.

Marshall watched Maksim cross the room to a blond guy who looked familiar. The man's smile and body language said he knew he could have anyone he wanted. Marshall cast a desperate look around. He needed to get out of there and drink himself into oblivion. It was stressful and depressing work being the coward Maksim accused him of being.

## CHAPTER TWO

Two weeks later...

Counting crunches became secondary to the dark hair and violet eyes Marshall couldn't stop watching. It had taken him fifteen minutes to decide if his eyes were playing tricks on him after spotting Maksim at the gym. Marshall had been going there for years. If he'd ever noticed Maksim before, he couldn't recall doing so. The man's dark hair kept falling in his eyes. It amazed Marshall that the man couldn't feel Marshall's stare. He hadn't looked away from Maksim since spotting him.

"That's Maksim Petrov," Trent said, cutting into Marshall's fantasies of having Maksim on his knees.

Marshall glanced over at his usual workout buddy at the words. "I know. We met a couple of weeks ago at a Blue Fires game. I was trying to decide why I'd never seen him here before."

Trent glanced Maksim's way. "Probably because he lives in New York. I think he's here as a guest of someone too important for us to ever meet. He travels a lot, so you know." Trent shrugged, as if Marshall could read his mind and finish his thoughts. "You should go say hi," Trent said, nodding Maksim's way. "He has a lot of connections. Waylon's out for this season, but when he comes back, he's going to want his starting position back. It can't hurt to know people like Maksim. He could be your ticket to a starting position with another team."

Irritation spiked inside him. "I'm not a user."

Trent shot him a dirty look. "I know that, but there's nothing wrong with knowing people."

"Mr. Frost," Maksim said, appearing at their side and rendering their argument pointless.

A smile tugged at the corners of Marshall's mouth. The same instant infatuation that hit him the first time he met Maksim came back with a vengeance. "Mr. Petrov."

"I thought I told you it is Maksim only."

Marshall bit the inside of his cheek, fighting the huge grin that tried taking over. "You did."

"Well, then, that's settled."

Damn, so much interest flashed in Maksim's gaze.

It left Marshall breathless. He couldn't look away, and he forgot where they were.

"Trent Goldman," Trent said, holding his hand out and saving Marshall from embarrassing himself.

"Maksim Petrov," Maksim said, accepting Trent's handshake.

"I'm a friend of Marshall's," Trent tacked on. "We went to college together."

Maksim's smile was different for Trent than it was for him. Marshall hated that he noticed, but he couldn't stop. When Maksim smiled at Trent, the gesture was friendly, but nothing more. The instant he shifted his focus Marshall's way, the man's smile turned wicked and full of intent. "I'm trying to be his friend, but he's still trying to decide if he wants me around."

Trent laughed as he slapped Marshall across the back. "That sounds like Marshall. He doesn't want you to think he's using you for your connections."

Marshall's mouth fell open. He turned an accusing look Trent's way. He couldn't believe Trent had said such a thing.

Maksim's laugh almost made his horror worthwhile. The man's eyes swam with mirth when he laughed. Marshall fought the urge to press his hand to his stomach to quell the butterflies. He'd never met a sexier man. "Perhaps I enjoy being used, eh?" Before Marshall could think of a response, Maksim turned serious. His eyes flashed with heat. "Besides, you are a very talented man. Perhaps I would be the one using you."

The Sahara desert wasn't as dry as Marshall's mouth.

Thankfully, Trent was full of words today. "He really is the most talented person I know," Trent said, sounding proud. "You should see his ground floor. The walls are lined with trophies. If Marshall touches a ball of any kind, he masters it."

Maksim's mouth lifted in one corner. "Is that so? Now that's something I'd dearly love to see."

"If you want to swing by when you leave here, I've got time." Marshall heard the offer as if it came from someone else. In fact, it took him a second to realize he'd definitely invited Maksim to come home with him.

"I'm headed out now. I just stopped by to say hi before I left."

Marshall couldn't let him get away. "I'm done too if you'd like to follow me out."

God bless Trent for not telling on him again. He was nowhere near finished with his usual workout routine. He'd let Maksim get away once. Marshall wasn't sure he could do it twice and still look at himself in the mirror.

"Sounds good."

At Maksim's agreement, Marshall came to his feet. Trent slapped him across the back again and winked before walking away. He focused on Maksim. "Would you like me to drive? Or would you rather follow me?"

Maksim motioned toward the door. "I'll follow you. That way I'll be free to leave in time for my afternoon appointments. Plus, I like bringing up the rear."

Marshall got the feeling there was a warning in there somewhere. He chose not to think about it too much. Even throughout his drive home, Marshall kept his mind blank. Thinking too much always got him in trouble. This one time, he'd let whatever happened happen. He was damn lucky Maksim bothered speaking to him again after the last time. This time, he'd do his best not to fuck things up.

———

"I'M IMPRESSED." MAKSIM WAS BLOWN AWAY BY more than just Marshall's trophies. His house was amazing for someone so young. The place didn't really have a basement, but it felt like it to Maksim, since they'd entered on the second floor. Everything was immaculate and polished. There was dark wood and some rooms smelled like leather. Maksim hoped, one day, Marshall would give him a grand tour of the three-story brick home. Well, another tour. One he would see. This time, he hadn't noticed anything other than the man leading him, because... damn. Marshall was beautiful. After their last meeting, Maksim never intended to approach Marshall again. Then, he'd been finishing up his final sets at the gym, and he'd felt the man's stare. When he'd turned his head, Maksim had lost his breath. Green eyes had been locked on him like a laser. With that one glance, Maksim had known Marshall would be the most amazing fuck. Attentiveness was highly underrated. Maksim had slept with enough men, so he knew exactly what made for the perfect experience.

Marshall effortlessly twirled a football on the tips of his fingers. "Don't be. Winning comes easy to me."

"I should think a lot of things come easy to you." Maksim couldn't help dragging his gaze down Marshall's body as he made the claim.

Without warning, Marshall tossed the ball his way. "Not everything."

Maksim easily caught it and threw it back. "Give me an example."

Marshall smirked but didn't bite. The playful glint in his eyes got the best of Maksim. Men liked to toy with him, but not the way Marshall did. This man was more like a giant child. He made Maksim want to be the same. When the ball came flying his way once more, Maksim snatched it from the air and hit the floor, as if taken down by the power of Marshall's arm. Marshall's laughter made the ridiculous move worthwhile.

Maksim felt lighter than he had in years, with no explanation other than being in Marshall's company. Marshall was easily a good ten years younger than Maksim, but the man's childlike nature was like a beacon, drawing Maksim in. A smile that felt out of control, even to him, stretched his lips. He turned his head and caught Marshall's eye. As he looked on, Marshall sprang, flipping onto his palms and walking across the room on his hands. Maksim wondered if Marshall ever acted his age. He hoped the man never grew up. While flat on his back in the middle of Marshall's playroom, Maksim watched as Marshall crossed the room on his hands, heading his way. A laugh escaped him when Marshall managed keep his weight balanced on his palms until he straddled Maksim's body. He slowly dropped to his knees, making sure he didn't harm Maksim. The man kept his weight balanced on his knees, sparing Maksim his bulk. The huge grin stretching Marshall's lips had Maksim wanting to kiss him just to taste the man's happiness.

"Are you always the jokester?"

Marshall shrugged. His bright smile never wavered. He was like a sexy man child. In fact, Maksim decided that would be his name from now on.

Maksim massaged Marshall's thighs. "Don't ever change, man child."

Marshall smoothed his hands down Maksim's arms before encircling his wrists and drawing his arms above his head. Marshall's dark expression had Maksim's mouth watering. He pinned Maksim to the floor by holding his arms down. When he leaned in, with their mouths inches apart, Maksim fought the urge to lift his head and capture Marshall's lips. Marshall had gone from playful and flirtatious to downright hot in an instant.

"Careful," Maksim whispered. "You're dangerously close to giving me the wrong impression again."

Marshall shifted, easily holding Maksim's wrists above his head with one huge hand. With his free hand, Marshall cupped Maksim's jaw and pressed his thumb to Maksim's lips, as if it was his lips instead. He nuzzled Maksim's neck. Maksim's dick strained to reach Marshall. Lust tightened his throat. He couldn't recall ever meeting anyone he wanted as badly. "You can't draw an impression if you don't think. Don't think," Marshall warned. The pressure against Maksim's lips increased as Marshall shifted positions, settling between Maksim's thighs. Marshall was hard for him—all previous impressions confirmed. Their erections bumped. Their thin workout shorts were no protection. They may as well have been nude. Maksim swallowed back a gasp, worried he'd spook Marshall if he made a sound. Marshall's lips brushed the shell of Maksim's ear. "We're just playing around. Two guys, tossing the ball." A ragged breath escaped Marshall. His hips rolled. The delicious friction against Maksim's erection had him leaking in his shorts. "Hanging out." Each word Marshall spoke came out harsher than the last. His hips rolled, making Maksim insane. He needed more, but he knew this would be the most he'd get. This was more than he'd dreamed Marshall would do.

Maksim's lips parted. Without thought, he touched the tip of his tongue to Marshall's thumb. To his surprise, Marshall didn't back down. He let Maksim lick him as he rocked against Maksim. With his mouth pressed to Maksim's throat, Maksim could feel Marshall sucking air while he fucked Maksim in his clothes. With his arms pinned, Maksim couldn't stroke Marshall, or himself. The pressure of Marshall's hips wasn't enough. Maksim had gone way past the point of caring if he came in his shorts and had to drive back to his hotel with a huge wet spot. In truth, Marshall wasn't touching him hardly at all. He didn't kiss Maksim or stroke him. His erection barely skimmed Maksim's through his clothes, yet Maksim had never been more aroused in his entire life. This boy drove him crazy with his I-don't-want-you but I-want-you attitude.

Maksim's balls drew up tight. Pressure beat at his crown. His hips lifted, seeking more. Seeking release. A chime rang through the house. Marshall leapt to his feet, looking unfazed. Maksim stared at him from his spot on the floor—dying.

"Someone's at the door. I'll be right back."

His words didn't make sense. Maksim's body screamed in denial. Marshall walked away. Maksim watched him go in confusion with his dick leaking in his underwear.

Marshall didn't come back right away. Maksim's body cooled. He rolled to his knees, silently cursing the sexy football player for teasing him. More than one set of footsteps stamped down the stairs. Maksim moved to the couch, grabbed the closest throw pillow, and did his best to hide his still half hard cock. Marshall, Michael, and Gavin descended into view.

A bright smile lit Michael's face. "Maksim. What an awesome surprise."

"Hey, it is the sexy Michael."

"Watch it," Gavin said behind him, sounding like the jealous husband he should.

Maksim winked, pushing his luck. "Do I lie?"

The pride in Gavin's expression had jealousy scratching at Maksim's skin. "No. You don't lie."

Michael saved Maksim from himself. "Marshall said he had company, but I never expected to see you here. Tell me everything," Michael demanded in his most scandalous tone.

Maksim might have laughed if Marshall didn't look so damn worried that Maksim might actually tell him everything. "I ran into Marshall at the gym. After listening to his friend brag about the huge number of trophies Marshall has, I had to stop by to see them for myself."

"Then we tossed the ball around," Marshall said, but no one seemed to hear him but Maksim.

Michael and Gavin's gaze stayed glued on Maksim. Gavin was the one who got the first word in. "Are you thoroughly impressed? Marshall's collection of trophies is massive. He's the best at everything he does."

Maksim's gaze slid Marshall's way. "It was worth the trip." He switched his attention to Michael before he gave Marshall away by the lust in his tone. "Now, I hate to run when you just got here, but I have a few practice sessions to attend today. I have my eye on some local players. It was nice seeing you both."

"You too," Gavin said.

"Don't forget you have my number," Michael reminded him. "You could let us know when you're in town sometime. Maybe we could take you to dinner."

"Sounds nice," Maksim said, flashing them both his most congenial smile. He genuinely liked Michael. The man was everything his twin was not—honest, for starters. Still, Maksim's gaze slid Marshall's way. Michael didn't set Maksim's body on fire the way his twin did.

Marshall wouldn't meet his gaze. "Thanks for stopping by. I had fun, showing you around."

"Thanks again for the tour," Maksim said, heading for the stairs.

Marshall followed on his heels. "I'll walk you out."

"You don't have to do that," Maksim argued. He didn't want to give Marshall away if Marshall was determined to lie to everyone, including his brother. "I can find the door."

The sexy-sounding chuckle behind him had Maksim's dick stirring again. He needed to get out of there. "I know you can find the door, but it's my house and my rules. In my house, I have some manners."

Maksim measured every breath as he climbed the stairs. He was hyper aware of how close Marshall was behind him. "Very well."

A half second before he reached the door, Marshall overcame him. His body molded against Maksim's and his lips touched the shell of Maksim's ear. "Damn, you have a sexy ass. I hate that we were interrupted."

Maksim's throat tightened. He'd never been hit so hard by desire. "Me too," he managed to squeak out.

Without warning, Marshall shoved his hand down the front of Maksim's shorts and stroked his hard cock. With that one move, he had Maksim ready to come in his pants. "Come see me again next time you're in town."

Because he couldn't make his voice work, Maksim nodded as he clawed for the doorknob. He had to get out of there. The man had company, so they wouldn't be fucking. Maksim couldn't see a second into the future past jacking off the moment he got back to the hotel. Jesus, Marshall fucked with his head. That wasn't necessarily a good thing. Maksim needed to find him a young, malleable, and hard-bodied athlete —one who'd be very grateful for his assistance in finding a pro contract. Those were always the easiest to please and leave. Maksim had a bad feeling in his gut that Marshall would be neither.

———

AFTER CLOSING THE DOOR BEHIND MAKSIM, Marshall pressed his forehead against the cool wood and gave in to the huge smile that had been trying to escape all day. He bit his bottom lip, trying to regain control. His brother was downstairs. Damn. Marshall readjusted his cock and made sure his t-shirt hid any hint of erection from sight before heading for the stairs.

He made a beeline for Michael and placed a noisy kiss on the man's cheek. "Twin!"

Michael swiped at his face. "Clown." His expression turned devilish. "Maksim Petrov."

Marshall shrugged and grabbed the football he'd abandoned earlier. He twirled it on the tips of his fingers—like he always did when he was nervous. "He's nice."

"Marshall and Maksim. That's so damn cute, I want to engrave some silverware."

Without thought, he tossed the ball at Michael's head. Gavin snatched it from the air before it hit its mark. He tossed it back Marshall's way. "No hitting Michael because you don't like what he has to say."

Marshall dropped down on the couch. "It's not like that. Trent says he could be a great connection.

You know, in case I lose my spot on the team next season."

Michael gasped and hit him in the arm, showing a decided double standard. "You're using him? Fucker. You're better than that."

Even though it didn't hurt, Marshall rubbed the spot where Michael hit him for sympathy points. "It's not like that either." Marshall shrugged. "He's fun, and like he said, he just stopped by to check out my collection. I'm sure we'll never cross paths again."

Michael looked away and sniffed. "Sure. Lie to me. What do I know, right? It's not like I've ever seen what two people look like after making out. What else have you been up to?"

Marshall couldn't help his smile. His twin knew him too well, but since his brother was amazing, Michael gave him an out. "Same as always. Jet-setting, whoring, and drinking myself into an early grave." Marshall could tell he'd wheedled his way back into Michael's good graces by the way the man tried hiding his smile.

"You're ridiculous."

"But you love me," Marshall teased.

"I'm the only one," Michael grumbled.

Marshall's smile fell. "I know."

Michael hit him in the arm again. "Stop that. Everyone fucking loves you. It's sickening."

"It's the whoring," Marshall said, incapable of being serious for long.

Michael shook his head as if he didn't know what to do with Marshall. "I guess I'd better tell you why we stopped by before you give me details I can never unlearn."

"You mean that's not why you stopped by?" Marshall asked, trying to sound innocent. He moved before Michael could hit him again.

Michael huffed instead and got to the point. "Gavin has to give a speech at a charity event tonight. It's a black-tie thing and I don't want to sit there alone while he's doing his thing."

Fuck. Michael was already giving him the puppy dog eyes and Marshall fucking hated black-tie events. "Where and when?" Marshall asked, sounding petulant even to his ears.

Michael immediately perked up. "The Vandelier Center at eight."

"You owe me in a big way," Marshall said, because it was easier than admitting there was nothing he wouldn't do for Michael.

Michael's mouth twisted in an obvious attempt not to smile. "I love you, big brother."

Damn, the ultimate blow. Michael only gave Marshall that two-minute age difference when he felt sentimental.

"You've already gotten your way."

"I'm not sure that's true," Michael said, sounding sad. "Maybe later, you'll tell me about Maksim."

Marshall shifted to his feet. "Okay, that's enough of that. I have to get a tux and you need to get out," he said, attacking before Michael could get away. He tossed his brother over his shoulder and headed for the stairs.

Michael's laughter let him know he wasn't pissed about the manhandling. "You can't toss me around like this. We're grown." He tried pushing at Marshall's back to get away, without luck. "And my husband is here."

"Your husband is ready to leave so he can have you alone," Gavin said behind them, his voice heavy with laughter.

Michael went limp, purposely making it harder to carry him. "No one is ever on my side."

Marshall dropped Michael on his feet at the top of the stairs. "Drama queen. Go home so I can get ready to entertain you later."

Michael winked, letting him know he wasn't as upset as he pretended. "Thanks, twin. You're the best."

"I know," Marshall said, one-arm hugging Gavin before shoving them both toward the door. "See ya."

He didn't stop pushing until his back was leaned

against the closed front door. The smile stretching his lips was beyond his control. Marshall told himself it was his brother's antics making his day, but deep down, Marshall knew the truth. A sexy Russian was to blame.

# CHAPTER THREE

Maksim had never liked public speaking, especially since his accent was thick and sometimes he didn't express himself well. His dislike didn't change the fact that he had more than most and a voice, so he did his part. With notes in hand, Maksim approached the podium while doing his best not to look at anyone in the crowd. Instead, he focused on the white tablecloths draped over hundreds of round tables and the low-lit candles flickering in the centerpieces. That way, it appeared he made eye contact with the crowd while he saw no one.

"Good evening. On behalf of the Thomas Handler Foundation, I'd like to welcome you to this year's Play for a Cure." A polite smattering of applause gave Maksim a chance to gather his thoughts. "As you all know, the Thomas Handler Foundation was founded by the wife of former football star Thomas Handler, after Thomas' tragic passing five years ago. Marie was rocked by her husband's unexpected suicide. Each year since, I've spoken on Marie's behalf, because the words are still too painful for her to deliver." Sympathetic sounds came from every corner of the room.

Maksim stayed focused on his speech. "After Tom's death, his autopsy revealed he suffered from Chronic Traumatic Encephalopathy better known as CTE. CTE is a disease caused by multiple concussions; concussions Tom suffered on the playing field. The damage done to the brain during these injuries changes the way a person thinks and feels over time. Sometimes to the point where they become a stranger to the people who love them most. In hopes of bringing something good from the loss of her husband, Marie has raised millions of dollars for research to find not only a cure, but new ways to prevent this same heartache from happening to others. For your two-hundred-dollar plate of food tonight, you're receiving more than a great meal with friends. You're saving lives." Maksim smiled, trying to lift some of the pallor from his speech. "Tonight, while you dine, we have several athletes and actors who've prepared speeches to entertain you. First up is New Orleans' best forward for the Blue Fires, and son of pro-football coach Jones Weeks, Gavin Weeks." Loud applause met with his introduction as Gavin stepped on stage. The man was a blond beauty with wide shoulders and flashing blue eyes. Maksim wasn't surprised people cheered for him. After shaking Gavin's hand, Maksim headed off stage to find his seat down front. Michael stood, making room for Maksim to slide past him and take the empty chair to his left.

"Great speech. I'm inspired to open my wallet," a low, sexy voice said close to his ear.

Maksim turned his head. Marshall sat behind them, their chairs brushing. The air caught in Maksim's throat. In a tuxedo and styled to perfection, Marshall was the hottest man in the room. Maksim couldn't look away. "It's the same one I give every year."

"I see why they keep asking you back."

Maksim needed to think of something else, anything other than this was the man who he'd jacked off to the fantasy of earlier. "I didn't expect to see you here."

"Michael made me come," Marshall said. His eyes swam with laughter. "If I'd known you would be here, I wouldn't have forced him to beg." Another round of applause went up, signaling the end of Gavin's speech.

Maksim clapped out of loyalty. He hadn't heard a word.

Marshall tugged on the back of Michael's jacket, snagging his brother's attention. "Now that your husband has done his part, can I finally go take a piss?"

Michael rolled his eyes. "Get lost. Sheesh, feel the brotherly love," Michael muttered under his breath.

While chuckling evilly, Marshall stood and tossed Maksim a wink before winding his way through the crowd and heading for the restroom. Maksim counted to thirty in his head before following. The restroom was empty except for Marshall, who leaned against a stall as if waiting for Maksim. His wicked grin had Maksim's feet moving. He hauled Marshall inside the stall and locked the door behind him before he found his back against the wall and Marshall overwhelming him.

Marshall buried his face against the crook of Maksim's neck and inhaled. The sensation against his throat had Maksim hard and ready to fuck. "Did you jack off with my name on your lips?" Marshall asked against Maksim's skin.

"You were amazing," Maksim growled, confirming Marshall's thoughts. He stroked Marshall's erection through his pants. Goddamn, the man was huge and rock hard. The noise he made when Maksim palmed him sent Maksim's heartrate through the roof. He didn't think he had much of a chance with Marshall. The man seemed untouchable in a way Maksim couldn't explain. He still couldn't stop trying. Maksim went in for a kiss. Marshall dodged him by leaning away.

A bland smile touched Marshall's lips. "I'd better get back to my seat before Michael realizes I'm a shitty brother. Up until now, I've been able to fool him."

Maksim matched his smile. "I get the feeling you're a damn good brother, but yeah. We'd better head back."

Marshall flashed him one final heated glance before checking to make sure they were still alone and slipping away. Maksim resisted the urge to bang his head on the wall since it seemed he'd never learn. He needed to stop trying to get the only man who didn't want him alone. There were plenty of good and willing men on the planet. Maksim would settle for one of those.

———

MARSHALL WEAVED HIS WAY THROUGH THE TABLES while trying to keep his erection hidden with his jacket. Even he didn't understand why he couldn't seem to stop playing with Maksim. Nothing good would come of it. Maksim was a dangerous game.

As Marshall slipped into his seat, Michael leaned his way. "Have you seen Maksim?"

His brain scrambled for a lie. He nodded. "I think I saw him in the bathroom as I was leaving, but it was crowded in there."

Michael bit his bottom lip. A line appeared between his brows. "I hope he hurries. It's almost time for him to take the stage again."

As if Michael's concern conjured him, Maksim appeared on stage, making Marshall wonder if there was some secret back entrance he didn't know about.

"Oh, good," Michael said, facing the stage.

Marshall bit back a chuckle. His brother was a handler for one the biggest actresses of the day. It didn't seem he could stop trying to keep people on schedule, even when it wasn't his place. Marshall's gaze shifted toward the podium. Everyone else disappeared. Maksim's lips moved. Marshall didn't hear a word the man said. Those lips had been inches away from his only moments earlier. The ache that hit Marshall, when he realized Maksim was about to kiss him, almost took Marshall to the floor. It scared him shitless how badly he wanted to taste Maksim's tongue. But there was no going back from there. If Marshall ever kissed Maksim, he'd never want to stop.

Maksim held his stare. For a moment, Marshall wondered if seeing the man's violet eyes locked on him was wishful thinking on his part.

Then Michael glanced his way before turning his attention back to Maksim. "Whoa."

Marshall tore his stare away from Maksim and focused on Michael. "What was that 'whoa' for?"

Michael moved in close, speaking against Marshall's ear where no one else could hear. "Look at the way Maksim's staring at you. He wants you bad."

"Nah," Marshall said, making light of Michael's claim. "I'm just another face in the crowd. Plus, he probably can't see a thing with all the lights shining in his eyes."

Michael shook his head. "I was up there earlier. He can see just fine."

Marshall couldn't think of another rebuttal. He didn't like lying to Michael, and it wasn't like Maksim hadn't made his interest clear. Marshall was scared as hell he'd open his mouth and his desire would pour out. Instead, he focused on Maksim with the same intensity the man showed him. He hoped Maksim would take the hint. Marshall might've dodged that kiss, but he wasn't opposed to letting the man try again.

# CHAPTER FOUR

With his shoulder holding up the wall and surrounded by reporters, Maksim watched Marshall give his after-game speech. While dressed in a business suit, with this hair still wet from his shower, Marshall looked downright lickable. When his boss had demanded his presence at tonight's home game against New Orleans, Maksim had scoffed but shown up. After all, it was his job to go where told, and he always had the best seats. After his last encounter with Marshall, holed up inside a bathroom stall, Maksim had sworn off the man. Now here Marshall was—on Maksim's New York home turf. Fuck, Maksim couldn't stop staring.

When Marshall stepped off stage, Maksim's feet moved in his direction. The man was immediately swarmed by reporters, and his coach stood at his side. Maksim couldn't stop heading his way. As if he felt Maksim's presence, Marshall's head turned his way. Heat flashed in the man's gaze before he quickly masked it. A smile that felt wicked, even to Maksim, pulled at the corners of his mouth. The way the crowd parted, easing Maksim's path, made him wonder if they'd been meant to see each other tonight.

"Mr. Frost."

Before Marshall responded, Coach Weeks who everyone lovingly called Coach, cut in. "I hope you're not here expecting to lure Marshall away. He's under contract."

He wasn't, but because he was a shark and damn good at his job, Maksim couldn't let the comment pass. "Contracts can be broken for the right number, but I'm here as a friend of Marshall's brother."

Coach brightened. "How is my son-in-law?"

Fuck. Maksim had forgotten for a crucial second that Coach was Gavin's father. "He's great. Last time I saw him, he still had that newlywed glow."

It surprised the fuck out of Maksim how proud Coach looked. He expected the man to deny any ties to a gay son and his husband, but Coach beamed with pride. "You noticed that too, huh? I was over there last weekend." He tapped his chest. "I got to meet

Mara King while I was there," he said, pitching his voice low as if it somehow hid his excitement over meeting such a huge Hollywood actress.

Maksim held on to his smile, hoping he looked impressed. "That's wonderful. If you can spare Marshall, I'd love to steal him away, and play catch up."

Coach's smile somehow brightened. "Sure. We're done for the night. As long as he's on time for our flight back tomorrow, he's free to do as he pleases until then."

Maksim switched his attention Marshall's way. "What do you say? I'd love to tell Michael I kept my word about showing you my town."

"How can I turn that down?" Marshall asked, sounding polite. There was no missing the glint in the man's eyes. It was the first time since they'd met when Maksim felt as if he stood a chance with Marshall.

He had to take a breath to calm his heartrate before meeting Coach's gaze again. "It was nice seeing you again."

"You too," Coach said, already focused on someone in the media.

Maksim stole his chance to slip away with Marshall on his heels. They managed to dodge any lingering reporters as they headed for Maksim's car.

When they reached Maksim's Audi R8, Marshall's steps slowed.

He eyed Maksim's blue baby. "This is nice." He flashed Maksim a boyish grin. "Okay, so I'm about to offend the shit out of you."

Maksim shrugged as he opened the driver side door. "Offend away."

Marshall waited to keep his promise until he sat in the passenger seat. "I didn't think talent scouts made R8 money."

An unexpected burst of laughter escaped Maksim. "They don't, and I'm not offended. Nice to meet you, Marshall Frost. I am Maksim Petrov of Petrov Energy Corp., the leading source of solar energy in the five largest cities of Russia. It's my father's company. Also, I am VP of Cyrillic Scouting Inc."

Throughout his speech, Marshall's expression never wavered. His mouth stayed lifted in one corner and his gaze remained locked on Maksim's lips. Finally, he met Maksim's stare and nearly blasted Maksim from the car with the heat in his eyes. "Nice to meet you, Mr. Petrov. I'm no one, but I'd still love to go home with you."

"You're far from being no one," Maksim said, shifting the car into drive. He would take Marshall home. Right now, before the man changed his mind again.

Maksim's apartment had nothing on Marshall's house, but apartments in New York were outrageous and hard to come by. Still, he had a nice corner penthouse with an amazing view and enough space for a single man living alone. He gave Marshall the grand tour, saving his bedroom for last. Marshall's stare never wavered from Maksim. Maksim's heartbeat sounded loud in his ears with each step closer to the bed. If anyone had ever made him feel more desired, he couldn't recall it. Marshall's eyes ate him alive. They shone bright with barely suppressed lust. It took every ounce of Maksim's control to move slow.

As they crossed the threshold into Maksim's bedroom, his lights flared to life before dimming to the perfect mood lighting. He never kept it bright in his bedroom. Maksim cast a quick look around his room, trying to see things through a guest's eyes. His huge bed was the focal point of the room, draped in black. It was funny Maksim hadn't noticed that before. He never brought anyone here. Maksim was the type to go home with other people or grab a quick tumble where he could. This was his private space. If someone got crazy or clingy, he didn't want them to know where he lived. Marshall was different. Maksim didn't know why.

"This place suits you."

Maksim didn't acknowledge Marshall's statement. Instead, he wrapped his arms around the man's waist from behind and unbuttoned his jacket before working it over his shoulders and letting it slide to the floor. "Tell me what you want," Maksim demanded. He was over playing nice. He kissed Marshall's shoulder and slid the buttons loose on his shirt while awaiting the man's response.

Thankfully, Marshall didn't play dumb or back down. "To be inside you."

Damn, Marshall sounded turned on. Unfortunately, Maksim was rarely a bottom and never to someone as flighty as Marshall. He *tsked*. "See, the thing is, you bang a lot of women, and I'm not sure that qualifies you to fuck me."

"I don't get fucked, so I guess we're at an impasse." Marshall's tone didn't leave any room for argument.

An evil smile tugged at Maksim's lips. "Hmmm, you could pass a little skills test," Maksim offered. He didn't doubt that if Marshall wasn't so turned on, he'd be gone already. He moved to the nightstand before Marshall came down from his high and walked away. Maksim came back with lube, condoms, and a masturbator shaped like an ass. Marshall eyed the objects as Maksim tossed them on the bed. "Prove yourself," Maksim taunted.

"Are you being serious?"

"It's not that hard, man child," Maksim taunted. "Every time you step out onto that field on Sunday, you have to prove yourself to eighty thousand screaming fans and millions of TV viewers. You've just stepped onto my playing field. Prove yourself." Since Marshall didn't look ready to run, and his tone hadn't lost any heat, Maksim didn't stop pushing. "You say you don't take dick and I don't take it from anyone who can't use it, let's do this. Unless you don't want me, that is," Maksim tacked on. It was a calculated risk. Marshall could still run.

A roar of triumph rang through Maksim's head when Marshall slid his belt loose and stripped. Marshall had an amazing body. The perfect quarterback body—one that could take a hit and stay upright. Maksim ate the man alive with his gaze, watching as Marshall suited up and lubed the toy. Marshall held his stare as he fingered the hole of the soft-rubber ass. Maksim's dick twitched, as if trying to get closer to Marshall. His heart raced and his mouth went dry. Marshall taunted him with what he could have. The man took his time, never blushing or backing down as he positioned the toy at the edge of the bed, set one knee on the mattress, and pushed his way inside.

Every muscle in Maksim's body tensed, as if it was his ass getting penetrated.

Maksim closed the distance between them, shedding his clothes as he went. His lips collided with the spot between Marshall's shoulder blades before he knew which move he'd make next. He needed to taste the sweat glistening on the man's skin. Maksim needed to feel the way man's hips moved as he slowly pumped inside the toy. He skimmed his hands along Marshall's body, savoring the way the man's muscles moved in the heat of passion. When Marshall moaned and his breath quickened, Maksim grabbed a condom and lubed up. He was a man who knew how to get his way.

Maksim started slow, massaging Marshall's ass cheeks. When Marshall didn't balk, Maksim skimmed the man's crack, pausing to toy with his asshole. Marshall leaned into Maksim's touch, as if silently asking for more. Maksim wouldn't go further without hearing the words. Still, he swiped his erection across Marshall's asshole, teasing them both while lubing the man's ass.

"Tell me you don't want me." Even Maksim heard the lust dripping from his every word.

Marshall's pants got louder. He fucked the toy while trying to get closer to Maksim's cock, but he didn't respond.

Maksim didn't back down. "If you want this dick, you have to say it."

A loud gasp filled the air, and Maksim knew Marshall was close. "I want you inside me," Marshall groaned.

He needed Marshall too badly to ask for more. Maksim pushed his way inside and quickly retreated. Sweat broke out across his forehead. If anyone had ever fucked Marshall, it didn't feel like it, and Maksim wasn't used to being gentle. A sound came deep from Marshall's chest and Maksim knew the window was closing to get inside Marshall while he was too distracted to feel the pain.

"Jesus, please?" Marshall begged, proving exactly how turned on he really was.

Maksim swiped more lube up Marshall's crack and impaled the man. The air left Maksim's lungs. He held still to keep from coming right then. Marshall was so hot and tight, Maksim saw stars. Then, Marshall exploded. His powerful orgasm milked at Maksim's cock. Maksim threw his head back and tried breathing through the pleasure, but nothing helped slow the rising ecstasy inside him. He pumped against Marshall's ass, riding out the waves as the most intense orgasm he'd ever experienced rocked him to his core. Maksim had known Marshall would be amazing, but nothing could've prepared him for this.

As they collapsed into a heap on the bed, Maksim held tighter to Marshall than necessary, but he couldn't stop. Marshall might get away if he did.

"I thought you were toying with me when you said no one fucks you," Maksim said between harsh breaths.

Marshall shook his head while gasping for air.

Maksim felt like a total ass for the way he'd handled things now that he realized the truth— Marshall had been one hundred percent honest about not messing with men. "Lots of men play games with me," he admitted, hoping to explain.

Marshall rolled in his arms and met Maksim's gaze, as if hanging on his every word.

Maksim gave him the truth. "They hope they'll win me, and I'll advance their careers. I am thinking I should apologize to you."

To his surprise, Marshall kissed him. It was light, at first. Their lips barely brushed. Then Marshall opened his mouth over Maksim's bottom lip and heat exploded through their kiss. Maksim found himself sprawled across Marshall, pinning the man to the bed as their tongues fought for supremacy. The heavy sensation in Maksim's chest was new. He tried not looking too closely at it. His mind shied away from what that feeling might mean. Right now, he had a sexy man in his bed. He had a good feeling they could be friends, and it had been an amazing night. Maksim was content with that.

————

MARSHALL WAS THE SAME GUY MAKSIM DESCRIBED. Trent had suggested Marshall get to know Maksim, in case he lost his position next season. It was no wonder Maksim couldn't trust anyone to be honest. Even he had failed. He was torn. Marshall knew in his heart he hadn't invited Maksim home that first time because of what the man did for a living. He also knew he hadn't let the man fuck him and he hadn't kissed Maksim because he wanted the man's connections. Yet there was still a niggling voice at the back of his mind saying he wasn't any better than anyone else Maksim had ever met. But he wanted to be. It was frightening how badly he immediately wanted to be special to Maksim. It was a fruitless hope. Maksim had made it more than clear that he didn't do strings. The knowledge held all Marshall's confessions at bay. There'd never be any reason for him to admit Maksim wasn't only the first man to fuck him, but he was also only the second man to kiss him. Years ago, he'd fucked a guy while overseas for a class trip—a man who didn't know Marshall and never would, but he'd never let the guy kiss him. In high school, he'd kissed Gavin, a moment that had almost ruined his brother's life.

Now, Marshall stuck with women while imagining himself with men. His career meant too much to him to lose it. Football locker rooms didn't care to entertain a gay man. In his heart, Marshall knew he was gay. It just didn't matter. He had too much to lose and nothing to gain. Maksim offered him kisses and more with no threat of altering Marshall's life. That didn't explain why Marshall's chest hurt each time Maksim's tongue brushed his. That had more to do with the way the man made him realize how much he'd lost to his career.

Maksim's fingers brushed through Marshall's hair. His kiss softened. "Stay the night with me," Maksim cajoled against Marshall's lips. "I promise no one will find out you were here."

He didn't need to think it over. Marshall nodded and deepened their kiss once more. The last thing he wanted was to leave Maksim's bed. He didn't want to face what he'd done or how it would transform his life. As much as Marshall wanted to believe nothing had changed, he knew better. The pressure sitting on his chest screamed nothing would ever be the same again.

# CHAPTER FIVE

Maksim: *Can I see you again? No strings, of course. You're free to look as straight as you like to the public eye. I'd just like to see you.*

Marshall: *I'd like that.*

Maksim: *I'll send you a pic of my travel schedule. We can compare notes.*

Marshall: *Sounds like a plan. Or, I could just come see you.*

Maksim: *Or, you could just come see me. I'll still send you the pic, though.*

Marshall: *Okay.*

———

THEY MET IN HOUSTON. AS MUCH AS MARSHALL

hoped to see Maksim sooner, their schedules didn't align until Marshall was due to play Houston on Sunday and Maksim had a Winger in his sights playing in Baytown on Thursday. Marshall flew in on Thursday morning to steal as much time as possible with Maksim.

He loved watching the man in action. There was a small twinge of jealousy in Marshall's chest, playing witness to Maksim's open flirting. Despite knowing it was part of Maksim's charm and how the man landed so many deals, Marshall wanted all Maksim's heated glances for himself. It wasn't fair of him, especially since Marshall pretended they were no more than friends. Still, sometimes Marshall's heart was stupid.

It was the first time Marshall had been to a closed hockey practice session. Considering he played for a pro-football team, and constantly practiced, he wouldn't have thought he'd find the event interesting. He was strangely entertained. The guys were jokesters and pranksters, but they got a lot of shit done. Maksim pointed out the player he'd been sent to acquire, Kentucky Armhill. Marshall had seen him play before. The man was large yet agile. Blond and godlike. Marshall didn't doubt for a second Maksim could and would have lured the man to his bed if Marshall hadn't tagged along.

As hard as Marshall tried not to listen to their

conversations during Kentucky's breaks, they were getting harder to ignore. While he leaned back in his seat with his arms draped across the backs of the chairs on either side of him, Marshall chewed his gum, kept a bland smile in place, and tried looking in every direction but Maksim's as Kentucky skated over.

The man's smile was huge. It was more than obvious he smelled a golden ticket in Maksim. "Did you see me check that guy? You have to come to our game Saturday night."

Maksim pitched his voice into a sexy growl. "You've got powerful hips. I'm sorry to say my schedule is already filled through Monday."

For once, Marshall couldn't look away. He kept his disinterested expression in place by force of will alone.

Kentucky's gaze slid down Maksim's body like a physical touch. "Then you should call me on Monday. I could fill your schedule until next Friday."

Marshall didn't stick around to hear Maksim's response. If Maksim planned to have Kentucky sliding right into his spot in their hotel room bed the minute Marshall was out the door, he couldn't know it. Speculation and wondering was one thing, but for sanity's sake, he couldn't fucking know it.

He came to his feet and pasted on his brightest

boyish smile. "I'm going to hunt down something to drink."

Kentucky's gaze slid his way. The man transformed into the guy Marshall imagined he was with every other straight guy he met—a man's man. "If you head up those stairs and take a left, there's a machine around the corner."

Marshall dipped his chin. "Thanks. You've got some real talent," Marshall added, somehow managing to sound impressed.

"Thanks, man. I appreciate it."

Without another word or looking back, Marshall jogged up the stairs and took a left. He had no idea what he'd been thinking by seeing Maksim again. Maksim could have any man he wanted, even guys Marshall had always thought were straight. All the excitement he'd experienced leading up to seeing Maksim this weekend turned out to be nothing more than wasted energy.

———

WITH HIS BOTTOM LIP BETWEEN HIS TEETH, Maksim forced himself to keep his gaze locked on Kentucky. His eyeballs itched with the need to watch Marshall leave. Staring after Marshall only had two outcomes: Kentucky would realize Maksim's interest was merely part of his plan to woo the man to New York, and Kentucky would recognize Maksim's true connection to Marshall.

"Your team captain is trying to signal you," Maksim said, nodding toward a group of men waiting for Kentucky to get back to work.

Kentucky glanced over his shoulder before meeting Maksim's stare once more. "All the guys want me," Kentucky said with a boyish smile.

Maksim held on to his faked good humor. All he wanted was to chase after Marshall. "I can see why."

"You planning on hanging around for a while?"

"We'll see. I have to make some calls, but we'll talk."

Kentucky winked and skated backward, heading toward his team. "Count on it."

The moment Kentucky turned away, Maksim's smile fell and his usual dissatisfaction with life set in. Marshall hadn't returned. Without looking back, Maksim followed the same directions Kentucky had given Marshall. It didn't take long to find the man, leaned against the wall in the hall. He had one foot resting on the wall and was playing on his phone. Maksim stole a moment to watch him. His gray t-shirt stretched across the man's chest, straining against his muscles. The way it fell, molded against his skin, showed off the man's six pack. One leg of his jeans was tucked inside his unlaced boot, highlighting how little care the man showed over his appearance. The flutter in Maksim's stomach said how much he loved it.

As he closed the distance between them, Marshall glanced up. Their gazes met and held. Maksim didn't slow. The hall was empty but not private. Maksim snagged Marshall's arm and kept moving, hauling the man along in his wake. He checked every door he passed until he found one unlocked. Maksim dragged Marshall inside. It was a supply closet of some sort. The door had a lock, and it was clean. That was all that mattered to Maksim. With them in no real danger of getting caught, Maksim shoved Marshall against the closed door and gave in to all the desire eating at his gut.

Since Maksim never knew if Marshall would kiss him, he went for the man's neck instead. He nipped at the cords and sucked at the man's pulse while tearing open the front of Marshall's jeans. Marshall was hard for him. His erection filled Maksim's hands.

"Goddamn."

At Marshall's harsh whisper, Maksim lost all semblance of control. He dropped to his knees. Marshall's cock filled his mouth. He sucked Marshall's dick like a man bent on tasting Marshall's cum. Ragged breaths filled the tiny room. Salt, man, and lust coated Maksim's tongue. It was his favorite concoction. Marshall's fingers tightened on Maksim's hair as Maksim swallowed Marshall's cock. He let the man have his way with his throat, encouraging Marshall's movements when his hips rolled. Maksim's dick throbbed, craving the sensation of Marshall's tight ass squeezing it. Nothing mattered more in that moment than Maksim's orgasm.

When the man came, a soft moan escaped him. Maksim's heart squeezed at the sound. He cared. Fuck, he had no idea why Marshall's pleasure mattered so fucking much, but it did. Maksim swallowed as fast as he could, needing every drop of Marshall he could get. Without warning, Marshall pulled him to his feet and captured his mouth. Their tongues fought. Marshall overwhelmed Maksim, attacking his mouth. Their kiss was almost desperate. Maksim cupped Marshall's face and stroked. Marshall's kiss softened. No matter how hard he tried, Maksim couldn't stop petting this sexy man.

"Jesus, I needed that," Maksim confessed. "I don't know how much more I can withstand of the child. All I want is to be alone with you."

"I'm a child," Marshall said, chuckling while still trying to kiss Maksim.

Maksim fixed Marshall's pants while stealing more touches. "You're a man child. That's so much better."

He tried backing away. "I need a moment. The last thing I want is for the young one to see me hard and think it's for him. I'm thinking his head is already swollen enough."

Marshall's smile was everything. "He's talented. I'm sure everyone has told him as much his whole life."

Maksim didn't want to talk about Kentucky any longer. He couldn't stop staring at the man's sexy green eyes. "Tolerate me for one more hour, okay? I promise my undivided attention will be worth it when I'm finished here."

Marshall's solemn nod had the tightness in Maksim's chest worsening. "Do your thing and don't worry about me. I agreed to come here, knowing you had to work. I'd rather have your divided attention than anyone else's fawning any day." His thumb brushed the line of Maksim's bottom lip. Marshall's eyes followed the motion. "You're fucking amazing."

Damn. Marshall meant every word. It was in his eyes. It wasn't an erection any longer that Maksim needed to worry about hiding. He was one hundred percent certain anyone who saw him would know— Marshall was breaking down Maksim's walls. He might not ever be the same.

———

WITH HIS MENU FLIPPED UP AND STRATEGICALLY placed, Marshall was free to stare at Maksim without giving himself away. He pretended to study each dish listed. In truth, his mind was deep in the gutter. Maksim had shed his suit jacket and tie earlier and rolled his sleeves to his elbows. A hint of chiseled chest peeked out from where he'd unbuttoned the top two buttons on his shirt. He looked relaxed and gorgeous. His dark hair fell across one eye. Marshall's palms itched to touch him.

"Do you see anything you like?" Maksim asked without lifting his gaze from his menu.

"A thousand things."

At his answer, Maksim's eyes finally shifted his way. His lips twisted wickedly when he realized Marshall stared at him. "I meant to eat."

"That too," Marshall said, biting back a laugh. With a sigh, he straightened in his seat and focused on the menu. "I'm thinking I'll probably get a steak."

"The world has never seemed smaller."

Marshall's head jerked up at the familiar voice. Michael and Gavin lingered at the edge of their table. Marshall's gaze shot to Maksim's. Maksim visibly struggled to rearrange his features and hide his surprise. Never in a million years had they expected to run into anyone in Houston. They'd gotten comfortable going out in public. To anyone else, they looked like two guys having dinner. Michael would know better.

Marshall came to his feet, determined to brazen it out. "Twin," Marshall said louder than he intended, drawing attention their way. He squeezed Michael a little too tightly. "What are you two doing in Houston?" Marshall asked as he one-arm hugged Gavin.

"I have a match against the Ice Devils tomorrow night," Gavin answered, patting Marshall's back.

A loud curse rang through his mind. When Marshall and Maksim had compared schedules and settled on Houston, it had never occurred to him to check who the Ice Devils were playing.

"I have a game here on Sunday," Marshall explained.

"Scouting," Maksim said, explaining his presence without waiting for anyone to ask.

"That makes sense," Michael said. His tone didn't match the way his gaze moved between them as if trying to put the puzzle pieces together.

"You should join us," Marshall said, hoping to pull his brother's focus away from the obvious.

Michael waved off his suggestion. "Nah. I'd hate to interrupt." He motioned between Marshall and Maksim, as if searching for the right term. "Whatever," he finished lamely.

"We're eating," Marshall said with a laugh. "And we haven't even started yet. It's crazy for all of us to be here and not sit together."

Michael looked at Maksim and then Gavin, as if assessing everyone's opinion before shrugging. "Sure."

After shuffling chairs, Marshall ended up next to Maksim. Their knees touched beneath the table. Marshall kept his features blank as he increased the pressure against Maksim's leg. His fingers found the man's thigh. The tablecloth hid his actions from sight.

"Who are you here scouting?" Gavin asked, oblivious to the drama playing out beneath the table.

"Kentucky Armhill," Maksim answered. To anyone else, his voice sounded normal. Marshall knew better. He heard the slight hitch as Marshall's fingers traveled higher.

Gavin nodded. "He's good."

Marshall fixed his gaze on his menu again, using the booklet to help hide the way he toyed with Maksim. He joined the conversation. "He's arrogant and favors his left side. If he gets picked up by a major team, he'll end up plagued by injuries. The man's already trying to hide a few." Silence met his response. Marshall glanced up to find everyone watching him. "What?"

"Have you been out scouting too?" Michael asked with a laugh.

Marshall realized how much he'd said with one statement. He shrugged, playing it off. "I watch hockey."

"You're good," Maksim said, making Marshall wonder if he meant good at assessing athletes or good at dodging.

"I wonder what brands of whiskey they serve here," Marshall said, wishing he was already drunk. What should've been an awesome night felt like it was turning into a nightmare.

———

MARSHALL ALWAYS PLAYED TO THE CROWD. Wherever he went or whoever he met, the man changed like a chameleon. Maksim had watched it happen all night and still couldn't decide how the man kept up with what everyone expected him to be. The idea made Maksim's head spin. The alcohol he'd consumed and the way Marshall had teased him beneath the table all night didn't help matters.

The hotel bed was a welcome sight. After getting ready to climb between the sheets, Maksim fell across the plush king-sized mattress and watched Marshall strip. The man disappeared inside the bathroom and returned minutes later wiping his face with a towel. Maksim's gaze slid down the tight body he craved. He was so easily swayed by hotness. All night, he'd been slightly aggravated over the way Marshall had handled things with his brother. He was even more irritated with himself for caring. Maksim had walked into this thing with Marshall with both eyes open. They weren't a couple. He had no right to demand Marshall stop pretending he was no more than a friend. Hell, maybe he wasn't more than a friend. Either way, he'd still spent the night angry. Now Marshall wore nothing and Maksim couldn't dredge up an ounce of vexation.

Maksim pulled back the covers and tapped the empty spot beside him. Marshall tossed the towel aside. His expression turned naughty as he climbed onto the bed and bounced like a giant kid. He braced his hand on the ceiling to keep from banging his head.

"Play with me," Marshall begged, sounding like the devil, tempting Maksim to sin. "Don't be scared," he added. "When was last time you jumped on a bed?"

"Never," Maksim answered as he ran his hand up Marshall's leg as high as he could reach. "You should come down here instead. I'll make it worth your while."

Marshall dropped like a rag doll, falling across Maksim, limp, but somehow managing not to hurt Maksim at all. Laughter caught in Maksim's throat as he shoved at the man's hard chest until he rolled onto his side next to Maksim. His eyes shone bright with mirth. Maksim's breath caught. Marshall's expression turned wicked. Maksim wasted no time smoothing his hand down Marshall's torso and palming the man's cock. It hardened in his hand. Maksim's mouth watered. Marshall rolled to his side, facing Maksim. With their faces inches apart, and Marshall's gorgeous green eyes watching him, Maksim broke. He kissed Marshall. A small part of Maksim still expected Marshall to pull away. Instead, their kiss was sweet. The tightness in his chest was back. Of course, sleeping with same person more than once was a new experience for Maksim. There was something special about Marshall. Marshall wanted him just because he did. The man didn't possess an ounce of avarice. He expected nothing from Maksim. The knowledge made Maksim want to give him the world.

He urged Marshall onto his stomach. Marshall went willingly, surprising Maksim. Maksim expected another argument about no one fucking him. Maksim was about to, except this time, he intended to take it easy—the way he should have the first time. Maksim's lips skimmed Marshall's spine. Marshall gasped. An evil smile tugged at Maksim's lips. Making Marshall writhe was addictive. There wasn't a doubt in his mind that very few, if any, men had ever explored Marshall's body the way Maksim intended to do. There was something empowering about that —like he was special. Marshall had held tight to his desires, never letting himself cave before Maksim. Maksim wanted to worship the man's body and honor his gift.

Maksim sank his teeth into Marshall's ass cheek while massaging the other globe. "Damn, I love your ass. Such a sexy man."

A ragged-sounding breath filled the air. Maksim did it again. He needed that noise caressing his ears. "I've never longed for anyone the way I crave you." Maksim slid his hand up the back of Marshall's thigh, massaging until he reached the man's ass again. He spread the man's cheeks and licked.

"Mak." The harsh way Marshall said his name drove Maksim on. He urged Marshall onto his knees. Maksim tongued the man's asshole, licking and dragging moans from Marshall. Marshall's back arched. He rode Maksim's tongue. Maksim dug beneath the blankets, finding the lube and condoms he'd stashed there when Marshall hadn't been watching. He kept Marshall on edge while prepping him to get fucked. The last thing Maksim wanted was for Marshall to come down from his high. With a condom covering his cock and lube coating the sheath, Maksim shifted onto his knees behind Marshall. He swiped his cock across Marshall's asshole, positioning himself. Marshall pushed back against him.

"Please?"

At Marshall's plea, Maksim froze. Marshall was the proudest person Maksim knew. Yet he humbled himself time and time again for Maksim. Maksim wanted to be a better person for Marshall—earn him.

Maksim gave Marshall what he begged for. He thrust, sliding inside. The sound escaping Marshall fucked with Maksim's heart. He wasn't supposed to care about this man who pretended to be straight. Fuck his life, he did. He cared. Maksim rocked against him, making love to Marshall. He kissed the man's spine. Licked Marshall's shoulder. Bit his skin. Marshall kept time with his movements. Every sound the man made screamed how much he loved what Maksim did to his body. Sweat coated their skin. Marshall jacked his own cock while Maksim fucked him. Pressure built in Maksim's balls and tightened his skin. He was so fucking close to blowing. His fingers found Marshall's hair and pulled. He licked the man's ear, surging toward the release his body begged for. Marshall's body tightened, squeezing

Maksim's cock almost painfully. A low cry bounced off the walls. Marshall's orgasm triggered Maksim's. Maksim gasped for breath as each wave of ecstasy hit. Even after the height of his pleasure passed, Maksim continued pumping inside Marshall. His heart refused to let the moment go.

"I can't get enough of you," Maksim confessed against Marshall's ear. His admission gave him the strength to collapse into Marshall, pinning him to the bed and holding him tight. "See me again," Maksim pled. He didn't know why, but Maksim couldn't let this man go. Maybe they'd never be more than they were now, but Maksim wasn't ready to let go.

"Just tell me when and where," Marshall said, easing the ache in Maksim's chest.

"Anytime. Everywhere," Maksim said, shifting where he could kiss the man who was under his skin. One day at a time. That was how he would win Marshall.

# CHAPTER SIX

M aksim: *Look what I found.*
    Marshall: *Is that a coffee mug?*
Maksim: *Yes. As soon as I saw your name on the back of the little football jersey, I knew I had to have it. I didn't realize it was a mug until I paid for it.*

Marshall: *That's awesome. Now I can be on your lips even when I'm not around.*

Maksim: *Exactly so.*

———

MARSHALL: *ANY LUCK GETTING HERSCHEL SIGNED with Ontario?*

Maksim: *You have no idea how diva-like some of these people are.*

Marshall: *Lol. Is that a yes or a no?*

Maksim: *I'm still not sure. It looks like I'll be here at least one more night.*

Marshall: *okay.*

Maksim: *I'm sorry. I know we had plans.*

Marshall: *Don't worry over me. You've never made me any promises.*

———

MAKSIM: *I HAVE A MEETING WITH KIERAN STEELE next Tuesday.*

Marshall: *Do you need a place to stay while in town?*

Maksim: *What I need is to see you.*

Marshall: *Done.*

———

MAKSIM: *DO YOU REMEMBER THAT KENTUCKY GUY from a few months back?*

Marshall: *The big-headed Winger? How could I forget?*

Maksim: *You were right. New York signed him and he's already out for the season with a leg injury.*

Marshall: *Maybe I should go with you more often to check out these players.*

Maksim: *I like this plan. You. Me. A hotel room with a jacuzzi.*

Marshall: *Let's make it happen.*

————

New Year's Eve...

Marshall: *What are you doing right now?*

Maksim: *Sitting here with a cup of hot cocoa and waiting for the fireworks over Park Slope.*

Marshall: *Sounds nice.*

Maksim: *It's cold as fuck. What are you doing?*

Marshall: *Sitting downstairs, enjoying the silence.*

Maksim: *Sounds lonely.*

Marshall: *It's not so bad.*

Maksim: *Can I call?*

Marshall: *I'd like that.*

————

There was something about the tone of Marshall's texts that had Maksim needing to hear the man's voice. Marshall answered on the first ring—like he was excited to hear from Maksim. The idea warmed Maksim's insides quicker than any amount of cocoa.

"Hey," Marshall said, sounding breathless.

"Hey, sexy. What are you wearing?"

A soft chuckle caressed Maksim's ear. He buried

the lower half of his face inside his scarf to hide his huge grin. "Workout shorts. I just got home from the gym ten minutes ago."

"Is that it? Just workout shorts?"

"Is that the only reason you called?" Marshall asked. "To find out what I'm wearing? If so, you should've FaceTimed me. I could've given you a real show."

Maksim had never been more thankful for his thick coat, hiding his instant erection. Even the cold couldn't douse his desire for Marshall. "I have faith you could talk me through the process."

"Hmmm, I don't know. You're in the park with cocoa. That sounds like some wholesome shit where you can't touch yourself."

Maksim was having the time of his life. "True, but I enjoy having my mind fucked too."

"Don't say I didn't warn you," Marshall said. His voice turned sultry. "The shorts are coming off. Don't scar anyone's kids. You still have time to change your mind."

"I'm all in, baby. Let me have it."

Marshall's dark chuckle had Maksim bracing himself. "I've been thinking about you all night."

"Have you?"

"Yep," Marshall said, sounding the same as when

Maksim fucked him. Jesus. This was torture. "Every place I look, I see a spot where you could fuck me."

"Maksim?"

Maksim jumped at the man's sudden appearance over his shoulder. He'd been so engrossed in his conversation with Marshall he'd forgotten he was in public. He turned to find Kentucky, hopping on crutches and smiling like they were old friends.

"Hi," Maksim said, sounding nervous even to his ears. It felt like he'd just gotten busted fucking Marshall in the park.

"Who is that?" Marshall asked. All hint of lust had disappeared from the man's voice.

"Kentucky."

"You haven't forgotten me," Kentucky said, as if Maksim had been speaking to him.

"Kentucky? Are you being serious?" Marshall asked. His irritation sounded loud and clear through the line.

"Unfortunately," Maksim said. He couldn't help the dry tone. This was bad.

"Wow," Kentucky said. "I wasn't expecting that greeting."

Maksim felt like a complete ass. "No," he rushed to explain. Maksim motioned toward the phone. "I'm having two conversations at once," Maksim explained. "That wasn't about you."

Marshall's sexy chuckle had Maksim ready to groan. "Liar."

"Oh," Kentucky said, brightening. "I didn't realize you were busy. I'll leave you to your call."

"It's okay, Mak. Go chat with the guy. He's probably down about being out for the season."

Maksim bit back a growl. "Hold on a second, baby." He moved the phone away from his mouth and focused on Kentucky. "Let me finish my call and I'll catch up with you in a few, okay?"

Kentucky's smile let Maksim know Marshall was probably right. The thing was, Maksim didn't want to spend New Year's Eve with a guy he barely knew. He wanted to be with Marshall. Plus, the last thing Maksim needed was for Marshall to think he was interested in anyone other than him. Sometimes he thought he might be winning the man's heart. Maksim didn't want to lose ground.

"That's cool," Kentucky said, motioning toward a spot nearby. "I'm hanging out over there with a few of my teammates."

Maksim flashed him a smile. "Be there in a few." He watched the man hop away before returning to his phone call. "So, are those shorts still off?"

"Sounds like you've got more men than you can handle tonight." Marshall didn't sound upset, merely resigned.

Maksim stared at his feet as he toed the ground. "I'm sorry."

"Don't be." Marshall rushed to reassure him. "I know I'm not the only..." Marshall stopped and didn't say anything else for a full five seconds, making Maksim want to scream. Finally, he sighed. "It's okay, gorgeous. Go. It's New Year's Eve. Have fun."

Maksim didn't know how to fix this, so he bailed. "Okay. I guess I'll talk to you soon."

"Sure," Marshall said, sounding like he didn't believe it.

Fuck. "Goodnight, babe."

"Goodnight," Marshall said, disconnecting their call.

Maksim stared at the night sky as he stuffed his phone inside his jacket. All he cared about was in New Orleans. He was stuck in New York.

Kentucky appeared at his side, startling him a second time. "I'm sorry. I didn't mean to interrupt a call with your man. How long have you been seeing each other?"

Maksim flashed him a quick smile. "It's okay. We've only been together a few months. It's long distance, so nights like this aren't easy."

Kentucky looked more solemn than Maksim ever imagined the man could be. "When you travel as much as we do, it doesn't matter where you live;

everything is long distance. Sometimes you meet someone worth it, though."

Despite the way the night had gone to hell, Maksim's lips turned up in the corners. "He's worth it."

"Then why are you here?" Kentucky asked. Curiosity dripped from each word.

Maksim shrugged. "By the time I got there, I'd have to head to Chicago the next day."

"So," Kentucky said, staring off into the distance. "That's twenty-four hours with someone worthwhile. That's more than some people get."

Maksim shoved his hands in his pockets and rocked back on his heels. He kept his gaze locked on the sky. No doubt he could see the stars in New Orleans. Not here. "I guess I should try to grab a flight."

Kentucky slapped him across the back. "Off with you. Tell Marshall I said hi."

Maksim's head whipped around at Kentucky's words. The man was already hopping away, stealing Maksim's chance to ask how he'd known. Fuck. All he could do was hope the man kept his correct assumptions to himself. Marshall would never forgive Maksim otherwise.

———

With his arms crossed over his chest, hoping to protect his heart, Marshall stared at his phone. Thirteen hundred miles away, Maksim was with Kentucky. Now that Kentucky played for New York, he lived in the same town as Maksim. He could be in Maksim's bed every night. The dude was out for the season. His life could revolve around Maksim. Marshall rubbed his chest. His heart hurt. Kentucky was sexy, arrogant, and secure in his sexuality. The man was everything Maksim deserved. Marshall didn't stand a chance.

He had no idea how much time passed while he stared at nothing and ached. Marshall sighed and stood. Maksim was single. Marshall couldn't stop him from fucking anyone else. He would take a shower and go to bed. Maybe tomorrow he wouldn't still feel sick at the thought of Maksim's name. Marshall let the water scald his skin. He stood under the stream until it turned cold. After turning off the water, Marshall didn't bother getting dressed. That was one of the perks of having no one love him. There was no one there to tell him to put on pants. He ran through the nightly routine of brushing his teeth and locking doors. Still, he didn't go to bed. Instead, Marshall paced the floor. Was Kentucky beneath Maksim yet? It was an hour ahead in New York. The fireworks would've flown, the ball dropped, and Kentucky had taken his place.

When a loud succession of knocking rang out, Marshall's gaze flew to the door. "Who in the hell?"

The knocks came again. Marshall checked the peephole. He bit his lip, trying to temper his smile. Maksim stood on the other side. Marshall opened the door, keeping his nudity hidden behind the wooden barrier. "You're here," Marshall pointed out unnecessarily.

Maksim's violet eyes shone bright with mischief. "I hopped the first flight I could—" Maksim's words died a swift death as Marshall closed the door. "Do you always answer the door in the buff?"

"Only for sexy talent scouts."

Humor filled Maksim's gaze. "That narrows it down a bit." Maksim's palm slid across Marshall's hip. "Damn. You're an amazing sight for starving eyes."

Marshall's cheeks ached. Happiness owned him. He couldn't stop smiling. "You're here," Marshall said again. There was no way Maksim could know how he'd appeared at just the right time, saving Marshall's sanity.

Maksim shrugged off his jacket and tossed it aside. "I couldn't stay away," Maksim confessed as he shuffled closer. His hands found Marshall's hips, towing him against his body. "I was standing there, staring at the light-polluted sky, waiting for fireworks I didn't care to see with Kentucky talking my ear off, and it hit me. I missed you, and there's no one else I'd rather be with tonight."

Marshall didn't want to be moved. He was scared to read too much into Maksim's claim. "I'm glad you're here," Marshall said, choosing to live in the moment. They were evenly matched in height. Marshall didn't have to move far to steal a kiss. He thought to be quick and move away. Then their lips met, and all bets were off. The uncertainty of where he stood with Maksim was always a stone in his gut. The only time the pressure eased was when Maksim touched him.

"I feel overdressed," Maksim said as he changed angles, coming at Marshall from a different direction.

Marshall went for the button of Maksim's jeans. "We should fix that."

With both of them tearing at Maksim's clothes, he was nude in no time. When their bare skin touched, Marshall sucked in a hiss. Maksim was cold to the touch from being outside, but he still set Marshall on fire. Maksim's kiss softened. The move punched Marshall in the heart. It was almost sickening how badly he wanted to call Maksim his. There was a hint of bitterness mixed with his longing because he knew it would never happen.

Marshall's lips moved to Maksim's jaw and then to his neck. Maksim palmed Marshall's hard cock. "Let's take this to my bedroom."

"I want to bend you over the couch," Maksim said, offering Marshall an alternative he couldn't resist.

"Oh, god," he breathed against Maksim's throat.

As if Marshall's desperation was the cue he'd been waiting for, Marshall found himself staring at the dark couch cushions with no clue how it happened. Maksim massaged Marshall's ass, teasing him. He heard Maksim rip into a condom. Marshall bit back a whimper. There was something about Maksim. The man possessed something no one else did. He made Marshall want to submit to his every desire. As Maksim pushed his way inside, making Marshall beg for release, Marshall realized something about himself. For the right person, he'd ruin his life. If Maksim ever decided he wanted to be that person, Marshall would give him the world.

———

FOR THE FIFTH TIME, MARSHALL BURIED HIS FACE in the crook of Maksim's neck and inhaled. Each time it happened, Maksim couldn't hold back his chuckle.

He adored moments like this—when Marshall let Maksim hold him.

"Why do you smell different?" Marshall asked, explaining the constant sniffing.

"A salesman shot me with cologne earlier before I could get away." He tightened his hold on Marshall. "I can't tell you what it does to me, knowing you can tell the difference—like you've memorized my scent."

Marshall's lips lightly brushed Maksim's neck. "You could blindfold me, and I could pick you from a crowd." Before Maksim had time to pull something stupid—like confess he was falling for Marshall, Marshall changed the subject. "What kind of place sprays innocent people?"

Shopping reminded him of something important. "A high-end department store near my apartment, which reminds me, I'll be right back," he said, climbing from the bed. Maksim found his pants in the living room and dashed out to the car. He was back with his bag in hand in a matter of minutes. After returning to the bedroom, Maksim stripped again before unzipping his suitcase. "I didn't get to see you at Christmas like I hoped." He pulled a red-wrapped box from his bag and held it out to Marshall. "I didn't get to give you your gift."

Marshall sat up and eyed the box. He didn't reach for it. "You bought me a present?"

Maksim shook the gift at him. "Yes. Open it."

After another heartbeat, Marshall finally accepted. He pulled the ribbon loose on top, gingerly unwrapping the present as if not wanting to disturb the paper. When he finally opened the box, Maksim held his breath. Marshall's expression was everything. The man had never looked more shocked.

"Holy shit. Is this really Nate Dyer's championship ring?"

"Yes," Maksim said, trying to hold back his smile. He loved making Marshall happy. "He sold it to a pawnshop some years back when he fell on hard times. Since I know he's your idol, I thought you should have it."

"Holy shit," Marshall repeated while still staring at the open box. "Now I'm scared to give you your gift. You've blown me away."

Maksim had thought his night couldn't get better after witnessing Marshall's reaction. He was wrong. Learning Marshall had gotten him a present too took his breath away. "You got me a gift?"

Marshall nodded and climbed from the bed. Maksim watched him cross the room with hunger in his gut. After setting the ring on his dresser, Marshall headed for the closet and came out with a gift bag. Marshall handed it over, looking nervous. "It's not a championship ring."

"I don't care if it's a tin of popcorn. You thought of me. That means more than you'll ever know." Maksim dug through the tissue paper. His fingers closed around something hard. Maksim lifted it from the bag. "It's a hockey puck." When he looked closer, he realized it was signed. "Wow. Is that Noah Cote's signature?"

Marshall nodded. "I know someone who knows someone."

"You must be joking. Noah rarely signs anything. Well, for adults. He signs shit for kids all time. His agent keeps tight tabs on him. This is amazing."

"Kieran can be a hard ass, but he's looking out for his clients' best interests. Like I said, I have a connection. Now you have another autograph to add to your collection."

Maksim stared at the puck, moved. "How did you know Noah was the only Phoenix autograph I was missing?"

"You mentioned it in passing once."

Maksim shook his head. He couldn't believe how amazing Marshall was. That was such a small thing to remember. Sometimes, Marshall made him feel important. Maksim slipped the puck back into the bag and set the bag on the floor before focusing on Marshall once more. "Thank you. That's easily the best gift I've ever received."

Marshall shifted to his knees and crawled toward Maksim, tumbling Maksim onto his back. He covered Maksim's body with his. "Let's see if I can improve on that gift while thanking you for mine," Marshall taunted. He kissed a path down Maksim's chest. Maksim closed his eyes and let his emotions take over. Soon, he'd be off to Chicago, leaving Marshall behind once more. This time hurt more than the other times he'd left. In fact, it hurt a little worse every time. Maksim feared that one day in the near future, he wouldn't have the strength to leave again. What would happen then? Marshall would never publicly claim Maksim, and Maksim couldn't be a secret forever. One day soon, this would have to end. The problem was, Maksim wasn't so sure he'd survive the loss.

———

MAY...

Maksim: *Can I stop by?*
Marshall: *You're in town?*
Maksim: *Yes, and I'd love to come over.*
Marshall: *The door's unlocked.*

———

Every time Marshall set eyes on Maksim, it was the same. The pressure on his chest, the way his breath caught, and the need to touch him always overwhelmed Marshall. The instant Maksim stepped through the door, Marshall overcame him. Their lips touched without as much as a friendly greeting. They were always immediate passion, burning hot and bright. Once Marshall's initial burst of possessiveness was assuaged, his kiss lightened, turning sweet. Maksim was really here. Marshall could touch him again. It had only been three days, but it felt closer to a year since the last time he'd seen him.

"Damn," Marshall cursed when he came up for air. "I've missed that."

Maksim stole another kiss before responding. "Me too. What's it been? A year? A decade?"

"Close," Marshall said with a laugh as he backed away, giving Maksim space. "Three days."

"You lie," Maksim said, sounding hot as his feet ate up the distance Marshall put between them. He claimed Marshall's mouth again. There was nothing sweet about Maksim's kiss. Marshall had no complaints. With one last nip at Marshall's bottom lip, Maksim finally set him free. Maksim pressed his hand to Marshall's chest and took a step back, as if forcing himself away. "I'm here on business."

"Business? Have you decided to start charging for

your sexual favors?" Marshall asked, laughing. "The first seven months of free tasting is over, huh? How much are you going to cost me now?"

Maksim's smile made Marshall's ridiculousness worthwhile. "It's nothing like that. If anything, I should be paying you." Maksim's expression turned heated once more. "How much do you want? I'd pay any price you asked."

It was on the tip of Marshall's tongue to demand exclusiveness from Maksim as his price. He barely stopped himself from allowing the words to fall. Maksim would never meet that price. Instead, Marshall chose to keep his pride. "We can come up with a mutually beneficial deal later. Now," he said, clapping once. "What business errand are you on?"

"Gavin," Maksim answered like ripping off a bandage. "New York wants him. They have for a while, and they're getting desperate. With desperation comes generosity and big bonuses."

Marshall didn't hesitate. "No."

Maksim didn't let up. "I've already spoken with Gavin on three separate occasions, making him offers, but he won't bite. I need your help."

"No," Marshall repeated. "Ask me for anything else that doesn't involve taking my brother away, and it's yours."

"I live in New York, and look at us," Maksim argued. "It wouldn't be stealing your brother."

Marshall knew Maksim really didn't want Marshall's opinion about looking at them. They fucked. Maksim had made that abundantly clear. They weren't a real relationship. Michael was real. Maksim couldn't have him. Michael was all Marshall had in the world. "He's more than a brother. Michael is my twin. That's something you can't understand unless you've had one. I won't ask him to move away."

Maksim's shoulders rose and fell as he sucked in a deep breath. His gaze never wavered from Marshall. "Okay. I'm not saying I'm giving up, but I won't ask for your help with this again. It's obvious you're set against it."

Now that Marshall had gotten his way, he felt like shit. He knew Maksim was just doing his job, but fuck. It was Michael. "It's not that I'm against Gavin getting a once-in-a-lifetime deal. I'm against losing the only family I have."

Maksim's open confusion made Marshall realize how little Maksim understood about Marshall's life. "You have more than Michael."

"Did I hear my name?" Michael asked, appearing in the kitchen doorway. He smiled when he spotted Maksim. "Maksim. It's good to see you."

"You as well," Maksim said, accepting Michael's hug.

"I feel like I'm seeing a lot of you lately," Michael said, as if digging for info.

"He's here to try to enlist my help in luring Gavin to New York," Marshall said without an ounce of guilt for throwing Maksim under the bus. Plus, he was still pissed over the man trying to steal his brother away.

"I hope you told him to go fuck himself," Michael said, making Marshall proud. "No offense," Michael added, flashing Maksim an apologetic smile. "My brother and my job are here in New Orleans. Gavin and I have a life here. That's why Gavin has already politely declined your offers."

Maksim held his hands up, showing his defeat. "Apologies. I'm just handling the tasks assigned to me."

For a moment, Michael eyed Maksim, as if assessing his earnestness. "It's okay. Anyhow," Michael said, switching his attention Marshall's way. "I'm here to grab that stuff from you. The memorabilia that you need Mara to sign for that charity auction," he clarified. "Mara plans to sign everything today, and then I'll bring it back by. She sends her apologies that she hasn't gotten to it sooner. The boys have kept her hopping."

"No problem. It's downstairs." Marshall headed for the stairs. Michael followed, but Maksim didn't budge. Marshall motioned for him to join them. "You coming?"

Maksim looked unsure of his welcome, but he joined them. Marshall found the box of donations for Michael while Maksim moved to the bookcase and inspected all the pictures lining the shelves.

"I cannot believe how alike you were," Maksim said, pointing out a picture of Michael and Marshall from their freshman year in high school.

Michael carried the box to the stairs. He eyed the framed picture as he passed. "Yep. Those were the days. If we didn't open our mouths, no one could tell us apart."

"Except Gavin," Marshall tacked on.

Maksim set the photo down. "I forgot he also grew up with you."

Marshall nodded. "We were inseparable when we were kids. Of course, I realize now he only hung around to be near Michael."

"I doubt that was the only reason he came around," Maksim said without looking his way. "Especially if you were as fun back then as you are now."

Michael laughed. "Marshall hasn't grown up much, if that's what you mean." Without waiting for a response, Michael focused on Marshall. "I'll back in a little while."

Marshall tossed his brother a wink. "I'll be here." Marshall waited until Michael was out of sight and earshot before focusing on Maksim once more. "So you think I haven't grown," he said, pushing up his shirt sleeves and flexing.

Maksim shook his head. "You're ridiculous."

Marshall dropped his arms and shrugged. "Probably, but you still keep coming back. So there's that."

"Of course I do," Maksim said, leaning closer to a different framed photo. "As I said, you're extremely fun. To fuck," he added, stabbing Marshall through the heart. He turned away before Maksim saw the hurt in his eyes.

"Who are these two extremely upstanding-looking people?" Maksim asked, drawing Marshall's attention to the framed photo on the bookshelf he'd been inspecting.

Marshall moved to Maksim's side, but he barely spared the picture a glance. "Those are my parents—Eugene and Helena Frost."

Maksim toyed with the frame, peering closer at the image. "They look... proper," he finally said, as if incapable of finding a better term.

Marshall bit back a laugh. He'd seen that photo a

million times. Marshall knew there wasn't a speck of fuzz on their thirty-thousand-dollar suits or a hair out of place. They'd smiled on cue and they were smiles they'd paid thousands to keep perfect. In fact, they'd probably practiced in front of the mirror every day. Proper was the most fitting description he'd ever heard of his parents. "There aren't two more flawless citizens on the planet."

"Why do you say that with such disdain?" Maksim asked. He crossed the room and stole a quick kiss before Marshall could answer.

Marshall shrugged. "They're closer to being proper citizens of the world than they are to being parents."

"You've never said anything, and I'm realizing now I haven't asked. Are they not accepting of Michael and you?"

A snort escaped Marshall. He didn't mean for it to come out sounding as derisive as it did, but there was no calling the sound back. "They'd have to see us to be unaccepting of anything. Michael and I are trophy kids."

Maksim's eyebrows drew together. "Trophy kids," he repeated, as if unfamiliar with the term.

Sometimes Marshall forgot Maksim wasn't always familiar with every American euphemism. "Yeah. You know, you get married, move to suburbia, and have two perfect kids. And we were the most perfect kids of all—twins. Our mom didn't have to do pregnancy twice. She did her duty, got her tubes tied, and went back to work. Michael and I got the best nanny money could buy until we were twelve and proved we were fine alone."

"I have a hard time believing your parents don't love you. You seem too well adjusted for that."

Marshall shook his head. "I didn't say they don't love us. They absolutely adore pulling out pictures of their perfect family to show their colleagues and potential clients. Growing up, I was the accomplished athlete while Michael was on track to be Ivy league—their future lawyer and business partner. Oh, and then Michael turned out gay. Fucking perfection," Marshall said, kissing the tips of his fingers for maximum obnoxiousness. "That gave them an in with a whole new community of folks. Look at our gay son; we'll fight for you too."

"So you don't see them at all?" Maksim looked confused.

Marshall shrugged. "They send us a card along with a huge check for every major holiday. Michael and I send them an expensive gift via a delivery service on Mother's day and Father's day. They get to show everyone their gifts and brag about their attentive and loving sons. We can say we have extremely supportive parents. A win for everyone."

"How big of a check are we talking?"

A sardonic smile tugged at Marshall's lips. "My parents aren't the sole supplier of energy to five major cities, like yours, but I could quit playing football right now and live a comfortable life. If I'm not extravagant and buy an R8, that is." Marshall honestly wasn't trying to bash Maksim having a family that drowned him in money. It was all the talk of his absentee parents making him obnoxious. Some things bit deep and turned bitter over time.

"Whoa. I know some lawyers make decent money, but wow."

Marshall waved off Maksim's claim. "Oh, my parents aren't just any lawyers. They own *the* law practice of the south. Everyone who is anyone uses Frost & Frost. They're on track to hold office someday. That's as long as their sons stay the adept and enduring soldiers they're paid to be. You know: no murders, drugs, or equally embarrassing incidents on our part. We have to stay who we are."

"The gay son and the athlete?"

"Exactly," Marshall said, flashing Maksim a bright smile for being the winner of the chicken dinner. "I smile for the cameras. Michael works for the top actress of the day. Oh, and he took home top prize for marrying an openly gay hockey star. We couldn't be more accomplished if they'd created us from clay, except we're not flawless, of course."

Maksim shook his head, as if he couldn't fathom the life Marshall described. Marshall didn't know how else to explain the life he led, and he'd already given Maksim more of himself than he'd given anyone else in his life. Sheesh, it was like the man didn't realize at all that Marshall loved him.

————

MAKSIM STARED AT MARSHALL IN AWE. HE couldn't believe how blasé the man was about being forced into a box that didn't suit him. The need to push and force Marshall to feel the rage Maksim felt on his behalf wouldn't subside. Maksim couldn't stop wanting Marshall to be real for him. "So, you're what? Throwing yourself on the straight grenade so Michael can be the gay twin?"

Marshall's nose scrunched up in the adorable way that always hit Maksim in the gut. "What? No. Michael is gay because he's gay. He doesn't need my permission or help."

All the irritation Maksim kept buried bubbled to the surface. "You just said you were trophy children and your parents might run for office—like you each played a role and you were forced into one that doesn't fit for your parents' sake."

Another ugly-sounding snort escaped Marshall. "I doubt they know anything about me beyond what I do for a living. Worrying over my sexuality is a form of concern. They don't do concern. And, what does my sexuality have to do with anything? You asked about my parents and I answered."

Maksim shook his head. He didn't understand why Marshall was so fucking blind. "Then why do you play at being someone you're not?"

Marshall's sweet smile almost made Maksim wish he could let this go. Then Marshall opened his mouth. "For the love of the game, of course. I've bled football for as long as I can remember. Why would I ruin a dream so few people have come true for five minutes of some dude's time, especially for some guy who doesn't do strings?"

Maksim chose to ignore Marshall's air quotes and obvious jab at him. "There are several openly gay hockey players. We're talking badass men who no one would dare pick a fight with on the street. It's not been an issue for them. It wouldn't be an issue for you."

An aggravated-sounding growl escaped Marshall. His eyes flashed with irritation. "That's hockey. Hockey has always prided itself on leading the pack when it comes to inclusion. I don't play hockey and football isn't the same. How many openly gay pro-football players do you know?"

Since this was important to Maksim, he took their conversation seriously and answered honestly. "I can think of three off the top of my head."

Marshall nodded. "Out of those three, how many are starting quarterbacks? Scratch that," Marshall said with a dismissive wave. "How many of those are starting quarterbacks who only have the position because they held down the sidelines as a second string until the starter got put out for the season? In fact, how many of those players are starters of any kind?"

A sad smile pulled at Maksim's lips. With every word Marshall spoke, he knew Marshall would never openly claim him. "I see your point. I guess, I just thought..." Maksim shook his head and didn't bother finishing. It was pointless.

Marshall's entire demeanor changed. His face hardened. "We can't all be you, Mak. Not everyone has a job that tosses us every semi-sexually confused up-and-coming athlete in the business that we can—literally—blow our way through. The rest of us are just trying to get through life with a little something to be proud of. I didn't change the rules here. You're the one who said you didn't do strings, and you didn't care who I lied to as long as I didn't lie to you. I'm not lying to you."

Maksim took a breath. He had changed the rules. Marshall had some right to his anger. "Okay, setting aside the fact that you may as well have called me a whore just then, I'm not asking... fuck." Maksim ran his fingers through his hair. Honestly, he didn't know what he was asking. He just didn't like the way Marshall made him feel sometimes. "I guess I didn't realize I would feel anything when you pretended for the hundredth time I was here on business when Michael stopped by. It's Michael, for God's sake. I didn't think I'd be a secret to everyone, including your brother."

Something dark passed over Marshall's features before his expression turned sad. Maksim wanted to kiss him and make his life easier. "I don't think you're a whore," Marshall said, sounding as sad as he looked. "You have options and freedom. There's nothing wrong with that. Plus, it's not like you made me any promises. But I can't bet my life and reputation on you. I can't put my heart and career on the line for someone who's made it clear I'm just a fun time. It was never my intention to hurt you or make you feel invisible. I don't want to hurt you. Maybe..." Marshall paused and cleared his throat. His face screwed up as if he was in pain. "I think, maybe we shouldn't see each other anymore."

"You think? Maybe?" Maksim needed more than that from Marshall.

Marshall held his stare. "I don't want to see you anymore."

Maksim drew back. He could beg, but he didn't know for what. He had been the one to say no strings. He'd been the one who acted like they didn't matter. Maksim could hardly expect more now. Their conversation had started out so innocently. All Maksim had wanted was to know a little more about Marshall's life. He'd never intended to make this about his unspoken feelings. In truth, he had no clue how things had gotten to this point.

He nodded while searching for something powerful to say. Something that would take them back to where they'd been before Maksim's feelings had gotten in the way. Nothing came to mind. "Of course. I mean, I never wanted to..." Maksim had nothing to say that wasn't a lie. He took a deep breath and pasted on a fake smile. It wasn't Marshall's fault he'd gotten attached. "Have a nice life, Marshall Frost. I hope you see your every dream fulfilled." Without looking back, Maksim headed for the door. He'd known things would end like this. The night he'd met

Marshall, he shouldn't have looked back when the man chased after him. He would've looked like a dick, but at least his heart would be intact. Now he'd have to relearn how to be a cold and heartless bastard. He'd have to relearn how to live without Marshall.

———

THE MOMENT MARSHALL HEARD THE DOOR CLOSE behind Maksim, he lost his shit. Nothing he possessed or could ever own mattered as much as what he'd just lost. His skin itched, crawling with self-hatred. Rage coated his vision. He'd never met a soul he'd been willing to lose everything for before Maksim, but what he'd said was true. Maksim didn't want strings and Marshall wouldn't settle for that.

Marshall's chest heaved, as if he'd run for miles even though he hadn't moved from the spot where Maksim left him. Anger boiled in his gut, making bile rise in his throat. His arm shot out, connecting with the glass enclosing his trophies. It shattered around him, biting into his skin. With the first blow and damage done, there was no going back. Marshall smashed everything in sight. This was all he had to show for his years on earth. Glass, plastic, and wood. Empty, cold awards. Trophies, just like him. He wanted them all gone. Marshall needed to be a clean slate. A slate someone might actually love.

When there was nothing left to destroy, Marshall calmly sat. He felt... empty. Marshall didn't kid himself. He loved Maksim. It happened when he wasn't looking. He hadn't meant to fall in love. Maksim had told him he didn't do attachments. Marshall had known from the beginning they'd never be a real couple. They had fun. From their first night together, it had been more to Marshall. He should've sent Maksim away a long time ago—saved himself. Saved Maksim. He hated his weak nature. Maksim was proud of the life he'd built. Fuck people's opinions. He made Marshall want to be the same. But Marshall couldn't make Maksim love him. He didn't know how.

The sound of footsteps on the stairs drew Marshall's gaze. Michael appeared. He froze halfway down. His gaze swept the room. "Holy shit." He focused on Marshall. His eyes were huge. "Oh my god, Marsh. What have you done? You're bleeding," he gasped, racing down the stairs to hover. He fussed over the open wounds and oozing blood Marshall hadn't noticed. Physical pain meant nothing. Marshall was numb to it all.

"I cleaned," Marshall said with a shrug while biting back a burst of hysterical laughter.

Michael's expression screamed he thought Marshall had snapped.

"Jesus Christ," Michael muttered, inspecting Marshall's cuts. He ran back upstairs, returning with a towel. Michael wrapped the material around Marshall's arm while Marshall stared at his brother's pinched expression. Michael tried pulling him to his feet. "Let's go. You need stitches."

Marshall's lips twisted. "Nah. Just leave it."

Michael struck without warning. His palm collided with the side of Marshall's head. "Stupid fuck. Get up. We're going to the ER. I don't know what the fuck happened, and you don't have to tell me, but you are getting off your ass and into my car. Let's go."

Marshall dutifully stood. It's not like it mattered where he went. Everything was gone. Maksim was gone. The knowledge rocked him on his feet, and he swayed. Michael reached out, steadying him. Marshall focused on his twin for the first time, really seeing him and his concern. Marshall's eyes filled with tears. Bending at the waist, Marshall set his hands on his knees and sucked air. His head spun. Maksim was really gone. Marshall had sent him away.

"Tell me what to do," Michael said, rubbing his back and sounding panicked. "Should I call an ambulance?"

"I told him I didn't want to see him anymore. Why did I do that?"

"Who?" Michael asked, justifiably sounding confused.

"Maksim," Marshall choked out. Even saying the man's name was like knives in his throat. "Why did I do that?"

Michael kept rubbing his back, as if that was the answer to everything. "Because you're a man, and a Frost. We fuck things up when our hearts are on the line." Michael bent and craned his neck, forcing Marshall to meet his stare. "You need stitches. So let's go get them. Then you'll find Maksim and fix whatever you've done."

Marshall straightened. "He's not looking for a relationship."

Michael led him to the stairs. "Well, he has one whether he wanted it or not. Get your stitches, and then get your man." Michael stopped at the front door and faced him. "And then you hang on, Marsh. No matter what you think people will say or do. No matter what you think our parents want. You hang on, because you deserve to be happy." He opened the door and paused. Michael glanced over his shoulder. "Oh, and for God's sake, stop fucking lying to everyone, including yourself. If you love this guy enough to do this to yourself, then step the fuck up and own it."

Despite everything raging inside Marshall's head, a smile tugged at his lips. "I love you, twin."

"Yeah, well," Michael said, throwing the door wide, proving how angry he was over Marshall's stupidity. "I'm not so sure how I feel about you right now."

Marshall's smile brightened as he followed Michael to his company car. Since Marshall worked out nonstop, and Michael was a small guy, they didn't look as much alike any longer, except for their faces. Those would always be identical. Marshall wondered if Michael had figured out that was why Marshall always called him twin. Michael was the person Marshall loved most in the world. He never wanted to lose their connection. If anyone had to see him at his worst, Marshall was glad it was Michael.

# CHAPTER SEVEN

Every gym in every town looked the same to Maksim. Some of them were bigger. Others were cleaner. But, for the most part, they were all the same. There were women and men who never seemed to do anything other than stare at themselves in the mirrors while there were others who grunted and dropped weights. Maksim preferred going late at night when the place was almost empty. He could be as gung ho or lazy as he chose without any witnesses. Plus, he hated waiting for machines.

Tonight, he'd chosen to go late for another reason —Marshall worked out here. The last time they'd ran into each other at the gym, it had been mid-day, and Maksim knew from spending time with Marshall, he was a morning person. Maksim needed something to do, but he didn't want to chance seeing Marshall. Three weeks without him wasn't enough fortification on his walls. He needed to rebuild his defenses if he planned to ever run into Marshall again. Right now, Maksim just hurt. Everything ached from the tips of his toes to his roots. Losing Marshall made Maksim realize how smart he'd been for avoiding entanglements before now. Nothing good came of caring. Maksim planned to never care again.

"I haven't seen you here in a while."

Maksim glanced up at the unfamiliar voice. The red-haired man looked vaguely familiar, but Maksim wasn't in the mood to chat today. "Yeah, I've been busy." Maksim stood and wiped down his machine.

The dude didn't let up. He followed on Maksim's heels to the leg press. "I'm Trent. Marshall's friend," he tacked on when Maksim didn't bite.

The memory hit. This was the guy who'd been working out with Marshall the first time they'd run into each other here. Hearing Marshall's name hurt. Maksim tried hiding it. "Sorry. I remember now. I meet a lot of people," Maksim added, trying his best not to seem rude. The longer he thought about it, the more Maksim realized this wasn't the only place he'd seen Trent. "Have I met you elsewhere? You seem familiar."

Trent lifted one shoulder in a half shrug. "I'm an on-ice official for the hockey league."

"Ah." There it was. Maksim had seen the man several times now that he thought about it. "Now I feel like an ass."

"Just for that?" Trent's friendly smile never wavered, but something in Trent's tone gave Maksim the feeling he'd walked into a trap.

Maksim was a smart enough man to know if he was in a hole to stop digging. He didn't respond. Instead, he lifted his eyebrows in question and waited for the other shoe to drop.

Trent's smile disappeared. He cast a look around, as if ensuring he wouldn't be overheard before focusing on Maksim once more. "I'd always heard you were a player, but you broke my boy's heart, and that ain't cool."

All Maksim could do was blink while his mind scrambled to catch up. There was no way Trent knew about Marshall. Not to mention, he'd been the one crushed in that equation. No matter how hard he racked his brain, Maksim couldn't figure out what was happening.

Trent snorted. It was an ugly sound. "Exactly how many dudes have you been fucking that you're still trying to decide who I'm talking about?" Before Maksim could dredge up a response, Trent made a dismissive gesture. "Jesus, don't answer that and give me more reason to be pissed. Do you have any idea how much Marshall risked on you? Personally, I don't care if you fuck everything that moves, but Marsh, he's like a kid in some ways. Making him think you cared was just cruel."

The shock of learning Trent knew about his relationship with Marshall rendered Maksim mute. He realized—in a detached way—there were arguments he should make. His brain refused to budge. Trent knew. He'd been certain no one knew.

"I've always called him my man child." For the life of him, Maksim had no fucking clue why those were the words that decided to pop out.

"That makes it so much worse," Trent said with a shake of his head. "Because that right there proves you know exactly what I mean." Trent walked away, as if too disgusted by Maksim to bother a moment longer.

Maksim went after him. It fucking mattered that anyone thought Maksim didn't care. For once in his life, he did, and it fucking mattered. "I love him," Maksim said, keeping pace with Trent. Trent stopped so fast Maksim nearly ran him over.

He spun. "What?"

"I love him," Maksim repeated, unashamed. "But

I'm tired of being his secret," Maksim added, putting everything out there. "I'd never ask him to risk his career or do anything he wasn't comfortable with. But I haven't spent my life fighting and working twice as hard as the guy beside me because I'm openly gay and they're straight, just to have someone fucking hide me."

Trent looked every bit as shocked as he should. Maksim never thought he'd love anyone either. Everyone knew he couldn't be tied down.

"I love you too."

Maksim's heart dropped into his stomach. Too late, he realized Trent's surprise wasn't due to Maksim's confessions as much as it had to do with Marshall standing behind him. Trent dropped his gaze to the floor and shuffled away, looking like a kid who'd gotten busted tattling.

Maksim's eyes fell closed. He took a deep breath before turning to face the man who'd ripped his heart out. Marshall looked like hell. There were dark circles beneath his eyes and his face was pale. He didn't look like he'd slept in forever. Maksim's throat burned. He wanted to take care of Marshall. The man needed someone who made sure he slept and ate. He needed someone to love him. Maksim did.

Marshall's gaze moved over Maksim's face, as if

trying to memorize him. Maksim knew the feeling. He'd never been more scared of never seeing someone again. "I don't know what to do," Marshall said, sounding as lost as he looked.

The pains in Maksim's chest made him wonder if this would kill him. "I can't tell you the answers. You have to figure life out on your own terms."

"You said you love me." Marshall's gaze continued moving over Maksim's face, as if searching for the truth.

"I do. You said you love me too."

Marshall nodded. "I do."

Each breath Maksim took came harder than the last. "There's always been strings," Maksim said, because he knew where he'd gone wrong. "Since that first night together, I've thought of you as mine, and I've been yours."

Marshall blinked and looked away for a second, as if Maksim's confession nearly broke him. He cleared his throat before meeting Maksim's gaze again. "Trent and Michael have known about you all along. You weren't a secret. I was just scared to let you have too much of me, because you didn't act like you wanted it."

God, they were stupid. Maksim cast a quick glance around the gym. It was late and very few people milled around. There was no possibility of them being overheard, but Maksim still couldn't kiss Marshall.

"I'm sorry," Marshall said, pulling Maksim's focus back to him. "It never occurred to me I was pushing you back in the closet," Marshall added, making it harder and harder for Maksim to withstand not touching him. "I understand if you don't want anything else to do with me."

"Fuck, Marshall," Maksim breathed, tilting his head back and seeking guidance from above. He blew out a loud breath before dropping his chin and meeting Marshall's stare again. The green eyes he dreamt about every night stared back at him, looking every bit as desperate as Maksim felt. Maksim couldn't take it. "You're a goddamn fool if you don't realize by now I'd rather be your secret than anyone else's husband."

Marshall bit his bottom lip, but deep lines appeared next to his mouth, as if he fought a smile.

Maksim held up a hand, stopping him before things went any farther. "But I'm not hiding in the bedroom if someone shows up at your place unexpectedly. I'm not thinking up some on-the-spot lie every time someone sees us in public. If you want to lie to people, that's on you."

"I love you," Marshall said, nearly bouncing on his toes.

"Damn," Maksim breathed before he could call it back. "I've missed my man child. Are we going home?"

Marshall held up one finger. A line of stitches running down Marshall's arm caught Maksim's eye. He didn't give Maksim time to ask about them. "Give me just a second." He stepped around Maksim. Maksim turned and watched him cross the room. As Maksim looked on, Marshall one-arm hugged Trent and said something against the man's ear before returning to Maksim. "I couldn't leave with him thinking I was mad," Marshall explained as he passed, heading for the door. Maksim stayed on his heels. He didn't know if this new arrangement would work, but he'd tried not loving Marshall, and that hadn't gotten him anywhere. Right now, he'd live in the present and take what he could. Being without Marshall was too damn hard not to try.

————

As Marshall walked through his front door with Maksim behind him, he didn't know what to do with his hands. It was an odd thought, but he wanted to touch Maksim and didn't know if Maksim would let him. Instead, he focused on the small things. He set his keys on the table by the door. He toed off his shoes. After that, he cast a desperate look around, searching for anything.

Luckily, Maksim didn't seem to have the same issue. "We should take a shower."

Marshall's gaze shot to his. Maksim looked so damn confident and secure—like he believed in them. "Yeah. I never got around to my workout, but it's been a long day."

"Can you get those stitches wet?"

Marshall twisted his arm and eyed the long row of sutures. "Yeah. I'm supposed to get them out tomorrow, so they're good."

Maksim's hand lifted, as if he meant to stroke Marshall's wound, before falling back to his side. "Do you plan on telling me what you did?"

"Something stupid," Marshall answered with a smile of embarrassment. "Let's just say, the cleaning lady won't need to dust my trophy case any longer."

Without a word or asking for permission, Maksim stepped around Marshall and hit the stairs. Marshall headed for the bathroom inside his bedroom. He kept his mind carefully blank as he fired the shower to life. Steam filled the room. Marshall pulled his shirt up and over his head. Warm lips touched his shoulder. Marshall's eyes fell closed. The smallest touch from Maksim always left him undone.

"Everything is gone," Maksim said against Marshall's shoulder as he wrapped his arms around Marshall's waist.

Marshall nodded. He knew how his ground floor looked now. Empty. "I lost you, and then I lost me," Marshall admitted. "You walked out the door, and I snapped. Nothing matters without you."

Maksim's hold tightened on Marshall. "It hurts my chest, thinking of all the irreplaceable things that were in that case."

Marshall turned in Maksim's arms and cupped the man's face between his hands. For a moment, he simply held Maksim's stare. He looked as tired as Marshall felt—like their souls were weary. Being without each other had drained them.

Maksim shoved Marshall's shorts down his hips, taking his underwear with them. "Get in the shower, man child. I'm about to fuck you."

———

MAKSIM FELT DEADLY. HE COULDN'T BELIEVE Marshall had destroyed all his trophies. Marshall was the playful one who always smiled. Yet he'd flown into a fit of temper and demolished all the things that meant the most to him. Maksim couldn't give that back to him. He wanted to spank Marshall for hurting himself. He wanted to comfort him. Instead of doing either, he stripped while watching the water slide down Marshall's gorgeous body.

Marshall watched him every bit as intensely. Neither of them would escape this encounter without teeth marks denting their skin.

Once he'd shed his clothes, Maksim closed the distance between them. Each step he took was measured. He was stalking Marshall, torturing himself with the thought of being inside this man who ate at his mind, enslaving him.

"I've met countless men."

Marshall blinked, looking like he'd been slapped. "Wow. I didn't need to hear that."

Maksim boxed Marshall in, crowding him against the shower wall. "You're the only one who's ever touched my heart. I've never told a soul I love them, but I can't stop wanting to tell you."

Marshall's expression softened. "Okay, that somewhat makes up for the oversharing."

"The idea of anyone other than you ever touching me again makes my skin crawl."

Marshall visibly bit back a smile. "I'm almost over your original confession."

Maksim palmed the man's erection. "It doesn't feel like you're angry to me."

"That's because my dick has belonged to you since the first time you touched it. You may as well put a little coat and tie on it and take him to work with you. That's how much you own my cock."

The darkness that coated his mind at seeing Marshall's destroyed trophy room disappeared. "How did I survive the last three weeks without your humor?"

Marshall's eyes fell closed. He visibly sucked air as Maksim toyed with his balls and fingered his asshole. "Damn, please tell me you jacked off a lot. That's the way I'm picturing you getting by."

With a chuckle that sounded evil even to him, Maksim pressed his lips to Marshall's chest and pumped two fingers inside Marshall's ass. "Yes, it was like that. Except, now that I've met a clown, I play with myself while watching stand-up comedy instead of porn."

As Maksim hoped, Marshall laughed. The sound died on a moan when Maksim urged his legs apart so he could milk the man's prostate. "God, you're such a tease."

"There's no condoms in this shower," Maksim

said, pointing out the obvious. "I want this sexy asshole squeezing my dick, but I have to wait. That doesn't mean you need to suffer. I love watching you come." Marshall sucked in a hiss when Maksim teased the sensitive nerve endings in his crown. "Your cheeks are flushed and you bite your lip—like you don't want to beg." Maksim leaned in and sucked Marshall's bottom lip between his teeth. He savored the sensation of Marshall's dick slipping through his fingers. "Every time you break, you steal another piece of my soul," Maksim whispered against Marshall's mouth.

Marshall shoved him away and dropped to his knees. All Maksim could do was stare down the line of his body as Marshall licked his cock from crown to root. Marshall had only sucked him once before. Maksim wasn't bothered. Marshall wasn't exactly the typical gay man. Now that Marshall had his lips wrapped around Maksim's dick, Maksim didn't know how to react. He loved coming while he was buried root deep in Marshall's ass, but he wasn't about to balk at the amazing blow job Marshall was giving. It had been his intention to tease Marshall until he cried for mercy. Now Marshall was the one in control. Maksim was at his mercy. He'd sign his car over to Marshall if the man asked in that moment. Marshall did something with his tongue that had

Maksim's eyes rolling back. He grabbed Marshall's hair and hung on. The pressure tightening his balls was just out of reach. It slowly crawled up his shaft. Maksim braced his palm against the wall, expecting his knees would give out at any time. A loud gasp reverberated off the shower walls as Maksim exploded. His vision darkened at the corners. Marshall didn't let up.

"I love you. Fuck. Marshall. I love you." Maksim heard himself rambling, but he couldn't stop. He fucking loved every little thing about Marshall and he would tear the world down before he let a single goddamn thing touch them again.

————

MARSHALL COULDN'T STOP TOUCHING MAKSIM. From the moment they fell into bed, exhausted and dripping, Marshall's hands wouldn't stop tracing Maksim's every line. Marshall kissed Maksim's shoulder. "I've been thinking," he said with his lips brushing Maksim's skin with each word. "I'd like to find a way to see you more often. Even though I don't have any clue how we'd pull it off, I'm between seasons, and I miss you when you're not around."

Maksim snuggled closer to Marshall's kisses, making Marshall smile on the inside. "Actually, I've been thinking about something since before everything went wrong."

The uncertainty in Maksim's tone had Marshall massaging every inch of the man he could reach, hoping to ease any worries he had. "Let's hear it. I want all your thoughts." The way Maksim's cheek curved let Marshall know he was smiling. Marshall had to kiss it. He placed tiny kisses below the man's ear until Maksim laughed. "Damn, I love that sound." Maksim's breathing hitched. Marshall's touch turned sexual. His playfulness disappeared as he lightly sucked the spot he'd been kissing. Marshall palm slid across Maksim's hip, heading for the man's cock.

Maksim spoke up, making Marshall forget his plan. "I'm thinking about starting my own scouting business. One where I could work and live anywhere —like here."

"Are you serious?" Marshall didn't wait for Maksim to answer. His excitement ran too deep. "Don't play with me now. Are you being freaking serious? You'd be amazing. With all your connections and your eye for talent, you'd be the number one agency in no time."

"Huh," Maksim said, sounding thoughtful. "At that first hint of your excitement, I thought your response was headed in a different direction."

Marshall urged Maksim onto his back where he

could meet the man's stare. "Why do you sound disappointed?"

Maksim's mouth lifted in one corner and he shrugged. "I guess I crave too much at times. It is not the money or success that has me wanting to take a new path. It's you. You're here. I wish to be where you are."

Marshall shifted positions until he settled between Maksim's thighs. With his chin resting on his hands crossed over Maksim's chest, he held the man's stare. "This idea of yours will give me exactly what I just said I wanted. You always give me everything," Marshall said with a shrug. "I'm proud of you. Let me be excited for your accomplishments," he begged, hearing the boast and need in his voice, but incapable of stopping. "You have no idea how much pride grows in my chest every time I look at you and know—somehow, for some reason—you chose me. I think you're amazing."

Maksim's heart was in his eyes. He brushed Marshall's bottom lip with his thumb. "Come here."

At Maksim's harsh-sounding demand, Marshall immediately complied. He loved Maksim's kiss. Hell, he just loved Maksim.

———

Maksim's throat burned. His eyes felt funny—like tears threatened to emerge. Marshall always made him feel more than anyone. When he'd tossed around the idea of freelancing or starting his own agency, he'd been scared as hell Marshall wouldn't want him around that often. At best, he'd hoped Marshall would be a little happy at the idea. Maksim never dreamed Marshall would react the way he did. He never imagined Marshall felt the way he did.

As their tongues brushed, so too did their erections. Marshall rolled his hips, as if slowly fucking Maksim. A moan rose in Maksim's throat. He wanted that. "You should make love to me, man child. I'd love to feel you inside me."

Marshall froze with Maksim's bottom lip held between his teeth. He released him and lifted his head. His gaze moved over Maksim's face, as if searching for any sign of doubt. Maksim knew what he wanted. The desire written in Marshall's expression deepened his longing to feel Marshall pushing his way inside, owning him.

"Do it," Maksim whispered, urging him on.

Marshall lowered his head once more and captured Maksim's lips. The man split his attention between stealing Marshall's kisses—lips brushing and clinging—and finding a condom. Maksim didn't move. He stayed still, letting Marshall take charge.

They were an odd couple—he knew. At heart, they both preferred to be on top, but they'd both equally surrender to the right person. They were each other's right person.

Marshall's lube-coated fingers toyed with Maksim's asshole. Since that was exactly what he was in the mood for, Maksim's dick leaked on his stomach. Maksim bit his bottom lip, holding back an orgasm. Need clawed at him. Marshall pushed his knees higher. The man's cock probed at Maksim's asshole. They held each other's stare. Marshall moved slow. His dick pushed past the ring of tight muscles. Maksim gasped. Goddamn, the penetration was everything he wanted at the exact moment he craved it. Marshall changed angles, ensuring he hit the right spot. Maksim arched into the man's thrust, needing everything. He sucked air through his mouth, fighting the urge to hold his breath and focus on nothing more than the pleasure. Maksim swore Marshall would kill him with ecstasy the way he moved slow and pumped deep. Goddamn, the man rolled his spine at the perfect fucking angle. No one had ever made him feel like this.

Sweat glistened on Marshall's skin. "I won't last long like this," Marshall said, sounding ragged. "You feel too good. I wasn't ready for how amazing you feel."

Jesus, Maksim's dick twitched and leaked like he was getting head. That was how much Marshall's words fucked with his mind. He couldn't take it. Maksim reached between them and tugged at his cock, needing relief. As much as he never wanted the moment to end, his brain screamed for release. It didn't take much. He'd been too close to the edge. A few short strokes had the pressure building inside him exploding into waves of spasms. Words and moans escaped him. None of it made sense. All he could do was feel.

A loud gasp rang through the air. "Oh, my god, Maksim. Jesus, I can't take it." A guttural sound escaped Marshall as the man's weight pinned him to the bed, pushing the air from Maksim's lungs. He didn't care. Oxygen didn't matter. They were more connected in that moment than ever before. Maksim's eyes stung. He'd never expected anyone to get under his skin. In fact, he'd taken several steps to prevent it. Maksim never once considered settling down. He always thought relationships sounded bland and boring. Being with only one person sounded stale. With Marshall, sex got better every time. They never got old. The more time they spent together, the more Maksim craved. He loved Marshall, and it happened so easily. Maksim already knew one day he'd wake up and refuse to ever leave

Marshall's side again. They were those soul mates he'd always heard about.

———

THERE WAS AN ODD VIBE TO THE ROOM—LIKE A hollowness. Marshall's eyes shot open. The bed was empty. He blinked at the spot where Maksim had been when he'd fallen asleep. The spot was smooth, as if he'd never been there at all. Marshall's stomach cramped. Had it been a dream? Maybe the constant pains in his chest—the ones that kept him up every night since losing Maksim—had finally sent him over the edge. His gaze moved to the bathroom. The door stood open and the light was off. Marshall's throat swelled. He couldn't climb from the bed and not see Maksim today. His spirit was too weary.

He rolled over and stared at the ceiling. His fingers connected with something under the covers. Marshall dug it out. The darkness that set in at finding Maksim gone lifted when he realized it was a note. How it had ended up under the covers, Marshall would never know, but he did move a lot in his sleep.

*Too excited to sleep. Went to work out.*

Marshall threw back the covers, and headed for the bathroom. Maksim was coming back. It hadn't been a dream. Marshall ran through his morning routine while trying his damnedest not to smile like a crazy person the entire time. He didn't bother getting dressed. There was no point. If Maksim was back, Marshall intended to haul the man right back to bed. Maksim planned to quit his job. He'd be here almost every day. The excitement had Marshall damn near jumping in place. He fought the urge to bounce from the walls. They needed a trampoline. That random and ridiculous idea carried him through his search.

A loud bang sounded from the ground floor, along with a string of Russian curses. Marshall jogged down the stairs. "I have an idea," Marshall said as he descended the stairs. "We should put a tramp—"

Three sets of eyes turned his way. The words died a swift death. Rage slammed into Marshall's gut. Trent turned his face away, but Maksim held his gaze with no shame. It was a ballsy move considering he had his foot resting in Henley Steele's lap. The man was married, for God's sake—to Kieran Steele—a man who'd ruin Maksim if he learned Maksim touched his husband. Not to mention, Maksim was his, goddamn it. "Did I miss a party?"

Henley stared at him like a deer in headlights. "Jesus," he breathed, eyeing Marshall from head to toe and back again, reminding Marshall he was nude.

"Guess who I ran into outside the gym?" Maksim said, his voice heavy with laughter.

"I thought I heard cursing. It never occurred to me you had another man down here, rubbing your feet."

A line appeared between Maksim's eyes. "I stepped on some glass." Before Maksim could say anything else, Marshall muscled Henley out of the way and took over inspecting Maksim's foot. Henley kept his face averted as he filled the empty spot next to Trent. The cut didn't look too bad, but Marshall didn't want it to get infected.

"I'll find you some antibiotic cream and a bandage."

"Why don't you find some clothes while you're at it," Maksim snapped, bringing Marshall's gaze back to his. Maksim didn't look happy.

"Everyone here has the same equipment. Why do you sound jealous?"

"Oh, no. Nope," Trent said, keeping his face turned away. "I can attest that we absolutely do not have the same equipment. Holy shit."

Henley stayed focused on Trent. "Right? I'm trying to forget having seen it. Otherwise, Kieran will kill me."

"Wait. I thought y'all belonged to that club," Trent said.

Henley shook his head. "We quit doing that."

"Huh," Trent said, sounding thoughtful. "It's been an informative day. The biggest BDSM couple I know has given up the lifestyle, and my friend should give up football for porn."

Henley grinned. His eyes swam with laughter. "Jesus. You're not lying. I'll never be able to look at him the same now that I know how ginormous his—"

"Are you two finished?" Maksim snapped, cutting Henley off. "That ginormous cock belongs to me." He focused on Marshall. "Go put some goddamn clothes on."

Marshall shook his head. Despite the situation, Marshall couldn't stop smiling. Maksim's possessiveness was hot as hell. He gently set Maksim's foot aside. After coming to his feet, Marshall leaned in and captured Maksim's lips. Trent already knew about them. If Henley hadn't, Maksim's jealousy and Marshall's nudity had cleared up everything. He knew Henley wouldn't talk. The man had his own set of secrets. In truth, Marshall didn't give a fuck about any of that. He loved Maksim. Maksim obviously loved him. He needed the man's kiss.

"Damn," Henley muttered. "Don't get him hard. I'm already jealous as hell."

"You're married," Trent argued.

"I'm not dead," Henley shot back. "And what about you? I thought you were seeing someone."

"Technically, but you're not supposed to know that. I don't want to lose my job."

"La, la, la. I'm not listening," Henley said, sounding like a kid. "Do not tell me a thing. If my husband is going to be forced to pull your ass from a sling for fucking a league player, I want to be able to plead ignorance."

While the two exchanged verbal blows, Marshall pulled Maksim to his feet and led him upstairs. He made sure Maksim didn't put any weight on his cut.

"Come on, sexy. I'll fix you up while they work out their shit. Then you can explain to me what they're doing here."

"Helping me set up connections for my new venture," Maksim said, clearing everything up before they even made it to the bedroom.

Marshall led Maksim to the bed and urged him to sit before searching out the first aid kit. He came back with what he needed. He gently cared for Maksim's cut.

"What were you saying about a tramp when you were coming down the stairs?" Maksim asked, laughing.

"We should put a trampoline downstairs now that my trophy case is gone."

"You say that like I'll be living here."

Marshall glanced up. "Maybe you will."

Maksim's amazing violet gaze stared at him, as if assessing his seriousness. "Maybe I will."

He definitely would. Maksim just didn't know it yet. Marshall fully intended to take over this gorgeous man's life—one giant leap at a time.

# CHAPTER EIGHT

**M**aksim searched through the junk drawer in the kitchen, looking for the scissors. He froze and stared down at the mess of Marshall and his things combined. They were living together. Maksim had no clue how it happened. He'd turned in his resignation letter, and his apartment was gone in the blink of an eye. Maksim called to let Marshall know his apartment sold, Marshall said they'd find a place for his stuff, and boom. Maksim couldn't find his scissors in a drawer filled with their stuff. Nothing was Marshall's or his any longer. It was theirs. Sometimes the knowledge hit Maksim at the oddest times. It wasn't shock or fear that froze Maksim in his hunt; it was wonderment. He'd never pictured sharing his life with anyone. He couldn't imagine being anywhere else.

"The infamous junk drawer," Michael said, appearing from nowhere and carrying catalogs. "You'll never find anything in there."

Maksim flashed Marshall's twin a smile. "Especially since there's twice as much junk now that I'm living here." He leaned over and kissed Michael on the cheek. "I didn't know you were coming by today."

Michael flashed the catalogs he held Maksim's way. "Yeah, this is the day Marshall and I spend every year, picking out what we'll send Mom and Dad for gifts this year. One day scheduling orders, and we're done with our familial duties until next year."

That was one of the most depressing things Maksim had ever heard. He kept it to himself. "Marshall is downstairs, studying game clips. Do you want anything to drink? I'll be down there in a minute."

Michael shook his head and opened the fridge. "I can get it. Go back to your hunt. You don't need to wait on me. Marsh and I have never been guests in each other's home." He froze and met Maksim's stare, as if his own words registered a second too late. "Wait. This is your home too now, and I just barged in without thinking. Would you like me to knock next time? If the door is locked, I usually do, but it was unlocked, so I assumed Marsh left it open for me. Now I'm realizing I just invaded your home and I feel like an ass."

Michael's rambling had Maksim's smile out of his control. There were moments—like now—when it was more than obvious Michael was Marshall's twin in more than looks. "Nothing has changed. This is still your second home. Come and go as it pleases you. Raid the fridge. Stay if you'd like. You are Marshall's twin. We love you."

Michael's smile let him know he'd said the right thing. Not that there was any other option. Marshall might not seem to mind the fact that Michael was all the real family he had, but Maksim minded. Sometimes it bugged the shit out of him that he was a trophy child, as Marshall put it. Other times, Maksim wondered if it was for the best. After all, he wasn't sure, if he was Marshall's parent, if he'd be the man he'd choose for Marshall. Not that it mattered. Maksim was the man who loved him. The man who'd love him until he died. Maksim's chest ached. He needed Marshall's kisses. He gave up on his search and hit the stairs. Nothing would be right again until Marshall's lips brushed his.

Michael glanced up as Maksim came into view. He smiled before going back to flipping through his catalog. Maksim moved in behind Marshall. His fingers brushed through the back of the man's hair before he thought about it. He tightened his hold and pulled, tilting Marshall's head back. He captured the man's lips. Maksim didn't consider his action. His need to taste Marshall eclipsed all thought. As their lips met, Maksim realized something huge. It was the first time Marshall ever kissed him in front of Michael. It didn't matter Michael already knew they were together and Maksim had moved in. Marshall had never kissed him with his brother as witness. Maksim was unprepared for the impact on his heart. He wasn't a secret. Marshall wasn't ashamed. They were a real couple. He was in love.

Maksim had to pull away to catch his breath. He'd never been so instantly winded. Michael was watching them and smiling.

Marshall scooted to the edge of the couch, making room for Maksim to climb in behind him. Maksim didn't hesitate straddling the man's back and pressing his lips between his shoulder blades. He stayed like that for longer than he cared to admit, inhaling Marshall's scent. The long-sleeve tight t-shirt Marshall wore kept Maksim from touching his skin the way he wanted. This was enough. He'd take it.

"I can't stop smiling," Michael said. His

expression matched his claim. "Seeing the two of you together makes my day."

"Where's your husband?" Marshall asked, ignoring Michael's statement.

"Off-season practice with some of his buddies," Michael said, sounding sad. Maksim felt a moment of connection with Michael. The man sounded how Maksim felt every time Marshall was out of his sight.

"What do you think about this for Dad?" Marshall asked, flashing the catalog Michael's way. "Last I heard, he was working on his golf skills."

Michael eyed the page. They were so matter of fact—like it mattered not at all that Marshall had heard through the grapevine his dad played golf and had never personally witnessed it. Michael shrugged. "Looks good to me. Maybe that along with a gold membership to White Plains Golf resort."

"That's good. I like that idea," Marshall said, flipping the page.

Michael turned some more as well. "By the way, Gavin says the rumors have started about you two."

Maksim's heart stopped. "What?"

Michael didn't look up. "Yeah. It's sort of like, is he or isn't he? Are they? That sort of thing."

Maksim felt Marshall shrug. "Let them speculate. Here's something else."

Michael glanced over and looked at Marshall's latest suggestion. "We got Mom that two years ago."

"Oh yeah." Marshall went back to his search.

Maksim still couldn't breathe. "I don't want to hurt your career." Maksim heard the soft confession as if it came from someone else.

Marshall glanced over his shoulder. "The only thing that would hurt me is losing you, so hush. Grab a catalog and get to work. This could take a while,"

Maksim bit his bottom lip and picked up a magazine. He wanted to argue. The last thing Maksim wanted was to ruin everything Marshall worked to achieve. He loved his man child too much for that. Maksim couldn't focus on the pages. He dropped the book. "Marsh—"

"I swear to god I will spank you if you say a goddamn thing that leads me to believe you have any intention of sabotaging our relationship because of some fucking true rumors." Marshall delivered his warning without once taking a breath or looking Maksim's way.

Maksim fought against his smile and lost. Michael caught his eye. The man's smile matched the way Maksim's felt. Michael winked before getting back to work. A few minutes and suggestions passed before Michael spoke up again. "I have another bit of news. How do you feel about being called Uncle Marsh?"

Maksim felt Marshall tense. His head turned Michael's way. Michael's gaze never wavered from his magazine, but the way he bit his bottom lip and smiled said it all. Marshall slapped the catalog from Michael's hands, leaving the man no other choice but to look at him. "Spill."

A smile exploded across Michael's face. "Mara's pregnant. She's agreed to be our surrogate. In about six months, you'll be an uncle."

Marshall flew to his feet and pulled Michael to his. "Shut the fuck up," he roared as he lifted Michael to his feet in a bear hug. "Oh my god. I can't believe it. Never in a million years did I think our family would grow beyond you and me. Wow."

"Congratulations," Maksim said, feeling an odd pang of jealousy. He'd never considered the life Michael so easily embraced.

Michael flashed him a quick grin before focusing on Marshall once more. "Gavin and I were wondering if you'd be our child's godfather? I know it's a huge thing to ask," Michael said, rushing out the words before Marshall could respond. "It's just that our parents aren't an option. Coach would do it in a heartbeat, but Gavin's mom hasn't spoken to him since he came out, and—well—you're kind of perfect for the job. I always thought you'd make one of those great, fun dads. Of course, we hope it isn't a role that ever gets called in, but the last thing we want is there to not be a plan in place." Michael finally stopped rambling. He seemed to hold his breath.

Marshall glanced Maksim's way. "What do you think?"

"I think it's none of my business," Maksim shot back without needing to think.

A line appeared between Marshall's eyebrows. "Of course it is. If there's any chance at all that a kid might come to live with us, that's your business."

Maksim's brain stuttered to a stop. Goddamn. They'd never felt more real. Marshall wasn't playing house. He'd moved Maksim in with every intention of permanence and they'd never even discussed it. Their love just seemed to eclipse all sense of reason.

"I'll let y'all think about it and talk it over. Just let me know sometime in the next six months," Michael said, reclaiming his seat.

Maksim didn't need to think about it. Chances were good that role would never get called in, but Marshall needed a family. Right now, all the man had was a set of shitty parents and a twin with a life of his own. This was one more tie. "It's fine with me," Maksim said quick before the topic slipped away.

Michael looked hopeful.

Marshall shook his head, as if in disbelief of how quickly things had moved. "Then I'd love to."

Michael popped back to his feet. "I think this calls for a round of beers and I need to call Gavin."

Maksim watched the man disappear up the steps. Marshall dropped to his knees between Maksim's and captured his lips before he had time to guess at his intentions. He had no idea how long their lips clung in the sweetest kiss they'd ever shared. All Maksim knew was he wanted all the silent promises Marshall made him with nothing more than the brushing of lips.

"The two of you are just so damn adorable," Michael said, reappearing with three beers in hand.

Marshall pulled away and flashed his brother a smile. He pretended to flip his hair. "What do you mean? I'm fucking adorable all the time. I'm like a baby squirrel on a hunt for his first nut."

An unexpected loud snort escaped Maksim. He shoved Marshall's shoulder, but the man didn't budge. "You're a fucking idiot," Maksim said with laughter heavy in his voice.

"Maybe," Marshall said, plopping down on his butt between Maksim's knees and accepting the beer Michael fetched him.

Maksim accepted his as well. He took a swig before pressing his lips to the shell of Marshall's ear. "You're my fucking idiot, and I love you." He watched Marshall's profile change. The shape of his cheek proved how big his smile grew. Marshall's happiness meant everything to Maksim. It was possible they'd never have all the things Michael and Gavin had. They'd probably never get married. He'd never thought about kids, but—most likely—that wasn't in the cards for them. Hell, Marshall might never publicly come out. Maksim was fine with what they had, because he had Marshall's heart. No other man on the planet could claim as much. He was content.

# CHAPTER NINE

The turf beneath his cleats was as much a part of Marshall as the color of his eyes. Even the sun beating down on him, burning his skin, couldn't dampen Marshall's love of the game. He'd worked twice as hard today, and he knew the reason. Maksim had joined him on the field today. With his new business up and running, Maksim needed new blood. Training camp was filled with players who were good enough to be pro but would still be cut from the team before the first regular season game. Maksim eyed each possibility. Marshall was hyper aware of his love walking the sidelines.

Two of Marshall's teammates, Will and Leon, stretched nearby. Marshall moved to join them. He grabbed a bottle of water and chugged it while fighting the urge to pour the entire bottle over his head. July was a tough time of year for training camp. The heat had dehydration setting in along with horrible cramps. They each tried taking as many breaks as possible to stretch and hydrate. It didn't help all that much. New Orleans in November was bad, but New Orleans in July was hell on earth.

"I've been meaning to tell you congratulations on landing the starting position this year," Leon said as soon as Marshall came up for air. "We all liked Waylon, but his arm is shot. Last year, we got closer to the big game than ever before. With you, we could make it this year."

Marshall fought not to preen like an idiot. He'd worked damn hard for this. It mattered that his teammates felt he'd earned it. "Thanks."

"Coach's son is here," Leon said, nodding toward the sidelines and changing the subject.

Marshall glanced behind him. Sure enough, Gavin stood, chatting with his dad. Marshall's gaze automatically slid Maksim's way. With a clipboard in hand, he walked the sideline. Marshall bit back a smile. Damn, Maksim looked sexy as sin.

Will snorted. "I see that Petrov guy is here too. Today must be invasion of the fa—"

Marshall's head whipped around. He dared Will with his eyes to finish his slur. "Go on."

Will visibly floundered. "Shit. Sorry. I forgot Coach's son is married to your brother."

Marshall fought his natural inclination to say it was fine. It wasn't. They were about to have a problem.

Will's shame lasted all of five seconds. "Speaking of which, why is he with that Petrov guy? Everyone knows that guy could get anyone a spot on the team of their choice for a blow job."

Something inside Marshall broke. There'd only been a thin dam between his head and heart to begin with, and Will's words were like a sledgehammer, breaking it down.

Marshall's spine stiffened. A smirk touched his lips. "Maksim isn't here with Gavin."

Will shrugged, looking nowhere near as concerned as he should. "What makes you think so? They're both gay, and—from what I hear—Gavin is a player. I'm just looking out for your brother."

There were so many things wrong with Will's statement, Marshall didn't know where to rage first. Instead, his wicked grin grew. "I know he's not here with Gavin, because Maksim is here with me." Without waiting to see the men's reaction, Marshall walked away, heading Maksim's way. He tucked his helmet under his arm as he went. His gaze never wavered from the man who owned his heart.

Maksim looked up from his clipboard. The man's expression turned heated when he focused on Marshall. "Hey."

"Hey, gorgeous," Marshall said before claiming Maksim's mouth. For a moment, Maksim stiffened in his arms. Then his hand landed on Marshall's shoulder and slid higher until he cupped Marshall's jaw. Nothing mattered except the lips against his and the man who owned them. For as many years as Marshall had spent worrying what people would think, it surprised him how easily that fear slipped away for Maksim. No one could claim he didn't belong on this team. If they wanted to win, they'd keep their fucking opinions about his personal life to themselves.

Marshall pulled away.

Maksim's gaze moved over his face. He massaged Marshall's neck. "You've done it now," he whispered.

"I don't care," Marshall said with a shrug and never meaning anything more. "You're mine, and you're worth it."

Maksim bit his lip and dropped his gaze to the ground before meeting Marshall's stare once more. The happiness written on Maksim's face let him know he'd made the right choice. "I love you, man child."

A whistle blew. Marshall glanced over. Coach pointed toward the field. "Get back to work, Frost."

With a nod, Marshall shoved his helmet on before tossing Maksim a wink. "Love you too. See you at home."

"Yeah. See you there."

Marshall jogged back onto the field without meeting anyone's gaze. He didn't fool himself by thinking his life would be easy now. In fact, he'd never been more certain things would never be the same. It didn't matter. He wouldn't spend the rest of his life hiding Maksim. If the shoe was on the other foot, it would kill him if Maksim denied him. The hard road was worth it, as long as Maksim was there to walk it with him.

————

THE WAY MARSHALL CARRIED HIMSELF—SO PROUD —was the sexiest act of defiance Maksim had ever seen. When Marshall kissed him, Maksim didn't know why the clipboard hadn't fallen from his numb fingers. He couldn't feel a thing beyond the shock. In the blink of an eye and with no explanation, Marshall put everything on the line for Maksim. Maksim couldn't tear his gaze away from the amazing man who'd ruined him for all others, even as the man moved to join the rest of his team on the field.

Gavin sidled up beside him. "Hands down, that was the bravest thing I've ever witnessed."

"Yeah," Maksim said, still reeling.

"Or the stupidest," Gavin added, pulling Maksim from his haze. He couldn't argue Gavin's logic. Marshall had said he wouldn't risk the life and career he'd built for someone who only saw him as a fun time. Maksim had let the man he loved feel that way for too long. They were in this together, and Maksim would never let Marshall go it alone.

"Man child."

At Maksim's shout, Marshall turned his way, but continued walking backward.

Maksim didn't need to think it over. "Marry me."

Marshall's face lit. "Tell me a time and a place. I'll be there."

"All the time. Everywhere," Maksim shouted back. His smile was out of his control.

"You're on," Marshall called out. He looked over at his teammates. Everyone openly watched their exchange. Marshall pointed at Maksim. "That's going to be my husband," Marshall yelled. The pride in his voice sent Maksim's heart soaring. Some of Marshall's teammates looked as if they thought he might be joking. Marshall shrugged when no one offered their congratulations.

For the first time in Maksim's life, everything felt right—like he was headed in the direction meant for him. Marshall had just given him the world, risking it all. No matter what happened, Maksim wouldn't let him down. No matter what, Marshall would be happy for the rest of his life, because Maksim wouldn't let it be any other way.

Marshall spread his arms wide. "I love you, baby."

A loud laugh escaped Maksim. Life with Marshall would never be boring. "Clown," Maksim muttered before pitching his voice for everyone to hear. "I love you too."

"All right. All right," Coach said, trying to call everything back under control. The man who looked like an older version of Gavin focused on Maksim. "If you want to stay, you have to let Marshall do his job."

Maksim pressed his lips together and nodded, thoroughly chastised. Soon enough he'd take his man home, where they could start their happily ever after. Until then, he'd have to be content with knowing he'd soon marry a good man who could've folded under the pressure of society's prejudice. Instead, he'd risked it all on love. That was who Maksim wanted at his side until the end of time.

# ABOUT THE AUTHOR

Charity Parkerson is an award winning and multi-published author with several companies. Born with no filter from her brain to her mouth, she decided to take this odd quirk and insert it in her characters.

*Seven-time Readers' Favorite Award Winner

*2015 Passionate Plume Award Finalist

*2013 Reviewers' Choice Award Winner

*2012 ARRA Finalist for Favorite Paranormal Romance

*Five-time winner of The Mistress of the Darkpath

Connect with her online:

--Join my street team: facebook.com/TeamCharityParkerson

--Sign up for my newsletter: http://bit.ly/CharityNews

--Website: charityparkerson.com

--Facebook:

facebook.com/authorCharityParkerson

facebook.com/TheMenofSin

--Twitter: twitter.com/CharityParkerso

admin@charityparkerson.com

www.ingramcontent.com/pod-product-compliance
Lightning Source LLC
Chambersburg PA
CBHW072238190626
46809CB00018B/2835